MURDER! THEY MEOWED

KRISTIE KLEWES

Murder! they Meowed

Merry Summerfield Cozy Mysteries, Book 3

Kristie Klewes

———

Ouch – an arrow in poor old Matthew Boatman's back! Not what I wanted to find when collecting for the Red Cross on a fine spring day in Drizzle Bay. Hoarder Matthew must have treasure a-plenty in his messy cottage because someone is prepared to kill him to get it. But what could it be?

———

For more information about me and my books, visit kristieklewes.com
Love and thanks to Philip for the unfailing encouragement and computer un-snarling... and to all my online friends who keep me company, poke ideas at me, and generally make life fun.
This is a work of fiction. Names, characters, places, and incidents are the product of the author's imagination, and are used fictitiously. Any resemblance to actual events, locales or persons, living or dead, is co-incidental. There are many beaches which could be Drizzle Bay, but let's just say it would be 'a short drive north of Wellington' if it existed.

1

PILED HIGH

I'D NEVER HEARD a whisper about Matthew Boatman being a hoarder. Dapper bespectacled Matthew – who always mowed his front lawn with a push-mower and was often to be seen clipping his six manuka bushes into perfect globes. Woe betide any rogue shoot that tried to spoil their rotund perfection!

I could always count on a cheery wave from him – or if it was summer and he was wearing a hat, he'd give me the kind of salute elderly men do by touching the brim without actually taking the hat off. He was the soul of politeness. A pillar of the community. Drove a really old car that was always gleaming clean.

It seemed odd on the Saturday morning I was collecting for the Red Cross that his front door swung slightly open when I knocked on it. Then a cat gave a loud and plaintive yowl from somewhere around head height. I took a step back with surprise – it was very close. I soon recovered and got my sense back though. It was only a cat, after all.

"Matthew," I called, pushing the door further open after he hadn't appeared for thirty seconds or so. "It's Merry Summerfield." Maybe he was in the bathroom? I gave him some more time in case, but nothing. Perhaps he'd popped inside from a snipping expedition to make a cup of tea somewhere out the back of the house?

The cat yowled again, making the hairs on the back of my neck rise up. What a spooky noise! A desperate noise – not a sweet little kitty-cat mew. Then there was a blur and a loud thump, followed by the rapid tattoo of furry feet on bare floor-boards. The cat had gone. But where had it been? I took a step forward, nose twitching, waiting for my eyes to adjust to the dimness.

It was very dark inside after the bright sunny day. Drizzle Bay in early springtime can be dazzling. Blue skies and hard, low sun. I took another step. Something crunched under my foot. Lordy, what had I damaged?

I bent down to see, and the light from the doorway behind me revealed the head of a small bird. Euw! Just the head. The body had been eaten, and a swirl of grey-brown feathers drifted along the narrow hallway. Narrow, I realized an instant later, because the walls on either side were stacked solid with old newspapers and magazines.

I'd never seen so many in my life. The head-high barricade ran past closed doors and blocked the access to those rooms. The cat must have been perched on top. No wonder it made a fair thump when it jumped down.

There were no other sources of light. No doors open, so no windows illuminating anything from the outside. No lamps on. Just my own long shadow stretching out in front of me, and a faint glow from the right-angled end of the paper-stacked space.

"Matthew!" I bellowed, spooked and weirded out. I didn't like the situation at all. My hair was up in a pony tail and the back of my neck chilled and prickled as the little hairs there rose further.

My yell brought no human reply, but another cat howled. I'm sure it was a different animal because its voice was low and hoarse and raspy – unlike the high panicked complaint from the first one.

This was fairly nasty. Should I check with the neighbors? I stood there dithering for a few moments, telling myself I was fully adult at almost forty-five, as tall as a medium-height man, well able to defend myself from a couple of cats, and had an open door only a few yards behind me if I needed to make a run for it. I swallowed, then pulled out my phone, turned its light on, and took a dozen resolute steps forward. What would I find around the bend? Something I could easily escape from – I hoped.

The heels of my fawn suede ankle-boots sounded loud on the bare timber floor and the soles made disconcerting rubbery squeaks. Matthew had no carpet, no rugs, nothing to soften the noise of my slow steps. I wrapped an arm across my waist to hold my jacket closed. It was cold inside the old house. Not to mention having that arm around me felt strangely comforting – even if it was my own.

I peeked around the corner just as at least three cats made a dash for freedom. Talk about a fright! My light made their shadows look enormous and distorted against the stacked-paper walls. They could have been tigers or panthers for all I knew.

A tail brushed past my leg, and paws raced over my feet and off down the hallway. I'm ashamed to admit I screamed. Only a short, surprised squawk followed by a bit of breathless panting, but still...

Matthew Boatman sat at the cluttered kitchen table, leaning at ease in his chair, a half-opened can of cat food in front of him. A can opener drooped from the rim. Why hadn't he answered when I'd called his name?

Then I saw it – a long, gleaming arrow neatly embedded in his back, right between the slats of the chair he was sitting on. It had taken me a few seconds to get far enough into the kitchen to see that. In fact I was fully into the room asking him if he was okay before I noticed it. He definitely had a strange expression on his face.

I imagine I did too. I gave a rip-roarer of a scream this time and bolted every bit as fast as the cats had, dropping my plastic Red Cross collection bag as I ran. The coins inside made a loud clunk on the floorboards and some of them escaped and rolled away into the darkness. I wasn't stopping to find them! Fresh air and sunlight were what I needed, and no dead people with arrows in their backs. The cheerful yellow jacket I'd put on to match the tubs of daffodils in the main street of the village suddenly seemed a very inappropriate choice.

I sagged against the black wrought iron gate, still panting, switched off my light, and scrolled with trembling fingers for Detective Bruce Carver's number. For once his snarky voice would be very welcome.

"Ms Summerfield," he grated, sounding surprised to hear from me. Well, it was several months since I'd told him he should go to Drizzle Farm and have a word with Denny McKenzie about the body on the X-shaped tree. Maybe he hadn't expected to hear from me again? For sure I hadn't imagined I'd ever find a third murder in our sleepy village.

My heart was doing the tango, pounding out an uneven rhythm somewhere behind the black lace Double-D cups of my new bra. I'd be willing to swear it was thudding right behind the little bow in the center.

"I'm in Paradise Road," I blurted. "Matthew Boatman's dead." Panting from my rapid run down the hallway and across the lawn – the shortest route to the gate – I added, "Shot in the back with an arrow." It was all I could manage.

There was absolute silence for a couple of seconds, and then DS Carver cleared his throat. "Hang on," he said.

I imagined him doing his 'turning on the recording gear' act and took the time to grab another couple of quick breaths. When I pressed my palm onto my chest I could definitely feel the way my heartbeat was galloping. What if I passed out from the fright?

Bruce Carver pulled me back to something like reality. "So, can we start again, Ms Summerfield – er, Merry? Where are you right now?"

"Leaning on his gate." And thank heavens it was there to lean on. My knees had started to tremble.

"Do you need medical help?"

Well, how nice of him to think of that! "No, I'm fine. Shocked of course, but not hurt in the least. Just a bit shaky."

He cleared his throat again. "I'll be there as soon as possible, but let's get a few facts gathered first. Matthew Boatman – in Paradise Road?"

"Yes. Number seventeen. The old chap with the super-tidy manuka bushes. I'm collecting for the Red Cross. He's on my list of streets."

Not that there are many streets in Drizzle Bay, but Lurline from the Animal Centre and Bailey Smedley – Lisa the vet's oldest daughter – and me and a couple of others, had divvied up the village between us.

"He's definitely dead?" Bruce Carver asked. "You don't need an ambulance for him?"

He hadn't seen what I had. How could he think I'd be mistaken? After all, this was my third experience of a breathless body.

"Definitely dead," I insisted. "And he might have been since yesterday because the cats are having to catch birds to feed themselves. He doesn't smell yet – well, no worse than the can of cat food he's trying to open."

DS Carver gave something that might have been a stifled guffaw. "Killed while opening cat food. That's a first. You provide me with interesting cases, Ms Summerfield."

That restored a bit of fight to me. "I don't *mean* to!" I exclaimed.

"Yes-yes, I'm sure you don't," he agreed, suddenly very conciliatory. "Okay, see you in about ten minutes. By chance we're just leaving Burkeville. Is there anywhere you can go and sit down? Your car, maybe?"

I should be so lucky. To sit in the cozy comfort of my Ford Focus – maybe with some music to soothe me – would have been wonderful. But no chance of that.

"It's a couple of blocks away at least," I said with a sigh. "I've been walking door-to-door." I grabbed a breath. "There's probably a low fence somewhere I can perch on. Bright yellow jacket, so you'll have no trouble spotting me." I bit my tongue to make myself stop talking.

After something that sounded like a couple of muffled door-slams he replied, "Right you are. We'll be there as soon as we can."

I should think so! Hanging about in the chilly open air for any length of time in my current fragile state didn't appeal. As that seemed to be all he wanted to know for now I disconnected, slid my phone into my shoulder bag, and looked around for a suitable fence. Although...

Thirty seconds later I was making my cautious way around the side of Matthew's old cottage. Maybe I should just make super-certain of what I thought I'd seen? But... hmmm... who imagines something like that?

I found the curtains were drawn at window after window – what a bind. There was no chance of seeing anything inside after all. But surely the kitchen had been light?

Determined to double-check myself, I kept walking slowly along, watching where I was placing my feet. Erring on the side of caution I made very sure I was treading on well-trimmed grass so I didn't leave any footprints in patches of earth to mislead DS Carver and his team. The soles of these boots have a distinctive zig-zag pattern and I didn't want him saying I'd overstepped the mark with my sneaky snooping.

But! My heart sped up. The kitchen window was one of those old-fashioned louvre-glass ones – fully open so the slats sat practically level. I found that curious – usually they'd be slanted downward in case of rain; ours in the back bathroom always are. I stared up at the slats for a few seconds. Five or six inches apart. Cats could get in and out that way if they were desperate, but there were no wisps of fur along the edges or paw-prints on the glass and it was a fair drop to the ground for them.

The table where Matthew Boatman sat was several feet

away from the window, thank heavens. He was wearing a dark brown woolen jumper, so mercifully any blood was more or less invisible. I didn't look too hard.

And I was only just tall enough to peer through the lowest gap. Even right up on tiptoe I couldn't have shot an arrow between the slats and into his back. But if I'd had something to stand on I could have managed it. And a bow with arrows of course.

Well, this was all very curious. Why were the window slats not tilted? I had a rummage in my bag and found one of my mother's old floral hankies – kept there for emergency sneezes. Folding it around the edge of one of the glass slats, I gave a little push. They moved – very easily. Had someone oiled the hinge mechanism to make them do that? They must have. Our window at home is as stiff as the creaky old door at the back of the garage.

Dismissing that thought I finally peered past Matthew and further into the kitchen. Holy moly, the place was a mess! I'd been so transfixed by finding him sitting at the table that I'd somehow missed the piles of cans and packets, the teetering towers of pots and casseroles, the big collection of random detergent bottles and cleansers, and all the stacks and stacks of what looked like brochures of weekly grocery specials on every level surface.

But of course once I'd seen that arrow a few minutes earlier, I'd turned tail and run without registering anything else. Can you blame me?

Shaking my head and shrugging, I pulled the window slats back down to where they'd been, made sure my hankie hadn't left any incriminating threads or smudges, and crept the rest of the way around the house. It was easier walking on the concrete path around the back, but then I started worrying about my boots leaving damp outlines there. I stepped out onto the grass again, hoping the sunshine and breeze would take care of that problem before the DS arrived.

Every further window was obscured by folds of curtains. What was the old boy hiding so assiduously? How much worse could the mess be than what I'd already glimpsed in the kitchen?

On the far corner of the house I found a small greenhouse where a few lettuces were doing surprisingly well for the time of year. The carcasses of dead tomato plants hung from the stakes they'd been tied to in the summer. I guess that was on Matthew's 'to do' list. Well, not going to happen now. On a shelf there were terracotta and plastic flower pots, neatly stacked. Hundreds of them. Many more than any sane person needed, and having seen the hallway and the kitchen I'd concluded old Matthew was maybe not quite sane any longer.

In a corner under the shelf, quite a sturdy box stood upside-down. Presumably not filled with dozens more flower pots. Would it hold a person's weight? Even a slightly too curvy and five-foot-eight person like me? I wasn't going to hang around and test it, but it looked a definite possibility.

There was a sliding door partly open, but as all the walls were glass I didn't need to push it any further to see everything inside. It looked to be a warm and sunny spot to judge from those crisped-up old tomato plants.

Maybe it was what I needed at home? A nice little greenhouse where I could grow a few vegetables without having them constantly bowled out of the ground by Manny and Dan? Honestly, the way Graham's dogs race around it's not worth having anything but the lawn and the trees.

While I stood there thinking about it one of the cats wandered over to see what I was doing (or more likely to see if I had any food). "Hello Peanut," I said. I received a plaintive meow in return. Peanut. Well, it was brown. A pretty cat, actually. Brown, striped, with a white chin. I've no idea where the name Peanut arrived from though.

I couldn't leave it and its friends unfed; I'm too tender-hearted for that, and anyway, a delicious scheme had just occurred to me – much more delicious than acquiring my own personal greenhouse.

"Hang on for a while, Puss, and I'll be back with dinner. I guess you might have seen what happened to your poor old master?" The cat mewed again, assuring me it had, and then rubbed against my suede boots to add a sprinkle of fur to the spaniel hair and anything else already there.

As I had no way of knowing how accurate DS Carver's estimate of ten minutes would be I decided I'd better trot out through the gate again and find an innocent place to sit until he arrived. A couple of properties further along I found someone had built a fence out of stones and boulders. They'd incorporated a seat big enough to take two people. Weird. Where had they got all the rocks from? Drizzle Bay is on a coast with hundreds of yards of sandy beach. And why had they bothered to make the seat at all? The view across Paradise Road is to a steep, grass-covered incline with the odd scruffy bush and fence post. Nothing to see there.

I lowered myself down onto the seat's bumpy surface with caution, making sure my tights couldn't snag on anything rough and my yellow jacket wouldn't come into contact with anything grubby. Honestly, the price of dry-cleaning these days!

It was just as well I'd removed myself from number seventeen because the DS's unremarkable grey saloon drew up less than two minutes later. Clutching a hand to my throat for a little drama, I stood, grateful to be off the stony seat. In fact I beat him to the gate. Or I should probably say 'them' because DC Marian Wick was predictably with him.

I unlatched it and pushed it open for them as though I owned the place.

DS Bruce Carver cleared his throat. "Might be useful fingerprints," he barked.

I tried to look contrite, but I guess he was right. Still, I'd had no idea about that the first time I opened it. "I've already come in through it and gone out as well," I muttered, "so you'll probably find more of mine than anyone else's."

He gave a barely suppressed sigh and waved a hand to

indicate it was 'ladies first'. I'd been thinking it was probably 'Police first'.

"How did you find him?" Marian Wick asked, eager as a fox terrier as we trooped up the crazy-paving path. "Where is he?"

A big shudder worked its way through me at the memory. "Sitting at the kitchen table. I was collecting for the Red Cross. I got such a fright I dropped my collection bag somewhere inside."

"So how did you get in?" she asked, striding along beside me on her runway-model legs.

Another shiver ran down my spine as we approached the door. Mindful of the fingerprint situation I didn't touch it. Instead, I pointed. "This was slightly open. The latch was fixed back, so I thought he'd probably been out in the garden and nipped inside for something. I called out. No reply. So after quite a wait I pushed it further open and called out again."

DS Carver glared at the house, took a pen from his pocket, and gave the door an experimental prod. I couldn't have told you on pain of death whether or not I'd automatically locked it behind me when I bolted out. Happily, not.

"I thought he might have been taken ill," I added. "He's not young."

"Did you know him well?" Marian Wick asked.

I shook my head. "Only to nod to if I was out walking Graham's dogs. Or some of Lurline's from the Animal Shelter. He was often in his front garden."

"So you went in?" DS Carver demanded.

I did my best to glare at him. Did he really think these rapid-fire questions would gain many people's co-operation? "Yes, of course I did. He's a hoarder."

That brought them both up short. Marian Wick turned and stared at me. She has huge, dark eyes to go with her long, slim legs. It's totally unfair.

"What's that got to do with it?" she asked. "Did you know beforehand?"

At that instant a cat shot out past the partly open door and bounded off into the garden and we all reared back.

"Not *another!*" I exclaimed. "There was one howling away inside while I was waiting. Then I heard a big thump as it jumped down from somewhere. That's when I pushed the door open and found this mess. And at least three more cats."

Bruce Carver turned back to the door and pushed it fully open. A waft of newspapery air greeted us, but thankfully no waft of cat. The strange dry fragrance of paper had struck me before, although at that stage I hadn't really registered its identity.

Knowing how dark it was inside the house I'd already pulled out my phone and turned the light on. I flashed it around for the detectives.

"Holy Toledo!" Marian Wick exclaimed.

"You're not joking," DS Carver agreed. "Okay, we have a better chance of securing the scene this time than we did at Saint Agatha's." He sent me a reproachful glare as though it had been my fault Vicar Paul had dashed around inside the church like a headless chicken before the forensics team arrived. Wouldn't you do a quick search in case the person who'd murdered the flower arranger was still there? And was maybe lining you up next?

"Is there a light switch?" I asked as Carver and Wick produced plastic covers from their pockets and slid them on over their shoes. "I need to find the Red Cross money I dropped."

"Stay right here please, Ms Summerfield," DS Carver commanded once he'd negotiated the stretchy covers. He'd be a lot more commanding if he had thicker hair, hadn't attempted to grow a goatee beard since I'd last seen him, and wore smarter shoes. "Your money will be recovered in due course."

"Can I at least have the plastic collection bag?" I wheedled. "The banknotes will mostly still be inside that."

"Evidence," he muttered.

"Only evidence that I was collecting for the Red Cross. I'm responsible for that money. Watch the bird's head," I added, just as Marian Wick stood on it. There was still a bit of crunch left.

Bruce Carver now had his phone out and was flashing its light over the walls. "No switch this end," he said. "Must be around the corner."

Marian Wick inspected the plastic cover on her shoe and shook her foot.

I pulled my jacket fronts closed, shivering much more

again from the awful situation than the air temperature. "Matthew's probably stacked the newspapers up past it. He's around on the far left. That's the kitchen. Everything else seems to be blocked off, but maybe he sleeps out the back somewhere? He can't just live in his kitchen. I was in too much of a tizzy to have a good look."

"Very pleased to hear that," Bruce Carver said. "Not that you were feeling bad, of course, but work like this is best left to trained investigators."

I held my tongue. I'd helped solve both the previous murders I'd discovered. No training at all.

I watched as they proceeded along the hallway, looking rather silly with their feet in the covers. Shouldn't they be wearing disposable overalls like the people in 'CSI' and 'Silent Witness'? Oh well, not really a worry. I was pretty sure the murderer had done it from outside and never entered the house. I couldn't see anything to steal. There was no way to get into any of the rooms without a massive clear-out in the hallway. You'd need a dumpster at the very least – not really something a thief would try arranging.

"If you find any footprints with a zig-zag pattern, they'll be my boot soles," I offered. "Once in and once out."

"Thank you Ms Summerfield," Bruce Carver said, bending to pick my Red Cross collection bag up off the floor. He took a few steps back in my direction and held it at arm's length so I could reach it.

I inclined my head graciously. "Some coins rolled out."

"We'll worry about those another time." He turned away.

"Sir?" Marian Wick called, presumably from the kitchen.

"Thank you for your help, Ms Summerfield," Bruce Carver called over his shoulder. Definitely a dismissal. I stared after him as he rounded the corner and disappeared. I'd lost all my enthusiasm for further door-knocking today.

2

FIG AND CHOCOLATE

I KNEW Bruce Carver and Marian Wick wouldn't be able to see me through the curtains (knew they couldn't even get into the rooms) so I ambled up the opposite side of the yard and stood staring at the greenhouse from the path. If the poor cats were suddenly homeless I could try asking Lurline Lawrence from the Animal Shelter to round them up and feed them and see about re-homing them, but catching cats is about as easy as pushing water uphill with a rake.

The greenhouse was on home turf. It was warm and dry to judge from those desiccated tomato vines. The sliding door, if I wedged it just a few inches open, would make it easy for the cats to come and go. It could become their base until they skedaddled away and found themselves new homes. Cats are good at that.

Of course I'd hatched a plan to stop off and feed them during my dog walks. What a great excuse to keep an eye on proceedings as the house was cleared out. They'd think I was being really useful instead of totally nosy.

I trotted around to the front door and waited, trying to look the soul of innocent helpfulness.

"Still here?" DS Carver demanded after answering my polite knock.

"I'm worried about the cats. I saw maybe four of them." I took a deep sniff. "At least you can't smell them in here. They must be house-trained."

DS Carver raised an impatient eyebrow.

"In fact nothing really smells, does it? Matthew must have not hoarded food or anything too gross."

The DS began to turn away. It was obviously time I got to the point. "There's a small greenhouse around the back," I said quickly. "It looks warm and dry. If you find any cat beds, let's put them out there and I'll come by and leave food for them each day until things get sorted out."

He breathed out rather noisily. "Ms Summerfield, I have bigger things to worry about than the murder victim's cats."

"Exactly!" I exclaimed, as though that was the most obvious thing in the world. "But they're living animals and need caring for. Let me take them out of your hair." I glanced up at his rather thin tonsure. Bad choice of words. He could do with a bit of furry augmentation, actually. "You don't want them getting in the way," I continued, "because this is going to be a massive clean-out job, isn't it?" I peered up the still-dim hallway. "How can anyone accumulate so much paper? How many years did it take him, do you think?"

"Cat beds," Bruce Carver muttered, ignoring my questions and glaring at me as though I lived in Drizzle Bay for the express purpose of making his life a misery. Yet another cat suddenly darted from parts unknown and skidded by into the open air.

"Sheesh!" he said, rearing back. "Fair point. I'll see what we can find."

I nodded. "You'd think there'd be a cat-door with so many of them. How have they been getting in and out?"

At that moment his forensics team arrived at the gate. It was with noticeable relief the DS shook his head and said, "No idea, Ms Summerfield. And now you need to excuse me. If we find any beds we'll put them out on the front lawn."

I'm sure I bobbed my head so enthusiastically I looked like one of those silly parcel-shelf animals you sometimes see in cars.

Great! I now had an excuse to come by again a little later because the lawn, although dry on top, would be damp further down. I needed to rescue the beds and get them re-located. Maybe put a sheet of plastic under them in the greenhouse to keep them dry underneath. Start a little trail of kibble across the yard to lead the cats to their new home.

Happy with my self-appointed role I waited until the forensics people had entered the house and then resumed my walk back along Paradise Road and past my car. I definitely deserved a cup of coffee and something nice to eat after my morning's good work and its horrible shock. Not that it would ever be enough consolation for something like that, but you do what you can.

My Dad, Arnold, was always a 'glass half full' person. He never felt things were beyond cheering up or improving. I got that from him. Life's basically okay – yes? Even when unexpected dead people turn up.

My brother Graham is the other way inclined. Quite convinced things can always get worse. Every 't' had to be crossed and every 'i' dotted, and even then some pesky detail might get away from him. He collects stamps – need I say more? Why does a grown man (and a clever one) get satisfaction from tiny squares of paper, sometimes with nasty inky marks on them? He'd get a lot more satisfaction from Susan Hammond if he'd only encourage her.

I slowed my fast clip as I reached the main street. The daffodils nodded in the sea breeze from their big tubs by the posts holding up the shop verandas. Saint Agatha's looked trim and tidy against its backdrop of dark green *pohutukawa* trees, and I thought fondly about Vicar Paul McCreagh (who might well give *me* some satisfaction if I really encouraged him). Behind them, the ocean sparkled, blue under the azure sky. Seagulls wheeled and screamed over the water. Everything looked so *normal* in Drizzle Bay. But once again, everything wasn't.

I wove through the thicket of tables and chairs outside The Café and sidled in.

Iona Coppington did a double-take when she saw me.

"What are you all dressed up for?" she demanded, eyeing my rather smart yellow jacket.

"Collecting for the Red Cross," I said, raising my official bag and waving it at her. (I should have locked it in the car, I realized belatedly). "Thought I might get better donations if I looked more respectable."

She tipped her head on one side. She always reminds me of a budgie or a parrot when she does that. I think it's her beady little eyes.

The Café was busy, it being a fine Saturday and late morning. I glanced around the tables, thinking I'd be lucky to get a seat. "I've been walking for too long. I need a sit-down and a flat white. And maybe a muffin." I peered into the glass display case where the kingdom of scrumptious had been set up.

Iona watched my face as my gaze roved across her baked goodies. "Cheese and bacon or fig and chocolate?"

She knew exactly which I'd choose! When had I ever bought anything savory from her when she had such delicious sweet treats available?

"Ummmmmm...." I said. "Fig and chocolate."

She smirked at my delaying tactic.

Of course I was itching to tell her about my gruesome discovery but there were too many people close by who might overhear. The announcement should come through 'official channels' after next of kin had been contacted, anyway. I knew that quite well, but I couldn't resist trying to extract a morsel or two of information from her.

"Does old Matthew Boatman ever come in here?" I asked as casually as I could. This didn't fool her in the least.

"Two date scones every Thursday." She drilled me with her birdy eyes.

I took a chance and asked a couple more questions. "*This* Thursday?"

She nodded.

"Morning or afternoon?"

"He's up at crack of dawn, that one. Always morning. What's happened?"

"Nothing... nothing..."

She sniffed. "Have it your own way, then."

I flicked glances left and right and leaned closer to her. "Can't tell you much here. Too many ears. Did you know he was a hoarder?"

Iona shook her head. "What? Piles of stuff everywhere? Did you see it when you were collecting?"

"Yes," I agreed, as though that was the news I was concealing. "His front garden is always so neat, but you should see inside that house."

"Smelly?" she demanded. Her eyes bulged at the thought.

Goodness, I mustn't wreck poor Matthew's reputation! "No, not at all," I assured her. "Well, a bit 'news-printy', I suppose. He must have newspapers back into the last century." There – that would give her a picture to consider.

"Wouldn't have expected that," she said, reaching into the cabinet with her tongs and making a show of choosing the largest of the muffins. Oh she's cunning – everyone always thinks they're getting the biggest because the person before them got the one that was even bigger.

I paid her and claimed a table that was just coming free as Lucy Stephenson picked up her bag to leave. Lucy is the local secondary school principal, and I've never seen a woman who looks so desiccated. She's thin to the point of emaciation, and her skin was surely made for someone much larger. Her face and neck are wrinkled all over, although her hazel eyes twinkle warmly from the network of furrows and lines. Supervising teenagers must be hell.

"I see the new basketball team's doing well," I said. "The vicar's whipped your troublemakers into shape?"

She sat again. "You saw the item in the Coastal Courier?"

"I did. And Vicar Paul told me they'd been going ahead in leaps and bounds."

Lucy gave a wry grin. "Shame they don't leap and bound into their schoolwork with the same enthusiasm, but yes – it's soaking up some of the energy and spare time the bigger boys have too much of."

"Can't be bad," I agreed. "Better they're reported for sports success than shoplifting or car theft."

She nodded, glanced at her watch, and then slung her bag strap over her shoulder. "Sorry – need to go. Promised to take Mother to visit the new exhibition in Winston's gallery before lunch."

I raised an eyebrow.

"Fiber arts." She rolled her eyes. "I imagine she's

expecting pretty crochet and he'll have chunks of salty old rope wrapped around pieces of driftwood."

Yes, I feared she was right. And with outrageous price tags attached. I smiled my agreement and nodded goodbye. I've no idea how Winston Bamber keeps his smart gallery solvent in a sleepy place like Drizzle Bay. We don't get *that* many tourists, but there he is, year after year, looking affluent and displaying such avant-garde stuff I can't imagine where it ends up. He once told me he had a big online presence, but even so...

A minute or two later Heather arrived with my coffee. Heather is Vicar Paul McCreagh's sister. She looks nothing like him with her blonde hair, blue eyes and pale English skin. Somehow he got the dark hair/all-year-suntan genes, lucky man.

Heather is also Iona's part-time assistant. And most importantly, she's the lady-friend of Erik Jacobsen from The Burkeville Bar. Honestly, you should see those two smoldering at each other. Why they're not at least engaged by now, I've no idea. When Paul and I were having brunch there in the summer, Erik asked Heather to change her return flight to England and stay longer.

"For me," he'd said, looking at her as though she was chocolate and Merlot and butterscotch all rolled up together. i.e. the most desirable woman on earth. This was in front of her brother and me, and John Bonnington who owns the other half of their business empire. Erik was serious, intense, and didn't give a damn who was listening.

She stayed, of course. Since then, no progress. Well, no ring on her finger, and no announcement of anything exciting. We're all still waiting.

I was halfway through my yummy muffin by the time she brought my coffee, pretending I wasn't eating it yet, but unable to resist pulling pieces off the sides and popping them in my mouth. Those nuggets of gooey dark chocolate and chunks of fruity fig were definitely helping to distract me from the memory of poor Matthew, skewered as he sat in his chair in the cluttered kitchen.

"Mind if I join you for a minute?" Heather asked, pulling out Lucy's empty chair and plopping herself down before I had time to say yes or no. Not that I'd have said 'no'. I couldn't stop myself from glancing at her third finger, left hand, though. Still no ring.

"Stop being so obvious," she muttered. "There are reasons…"

I couldn't help smirking. "*What* reasons? You must know we're all curious."

She pushed a few loose sugar grains into the middle of the table with her forefinger. "And you're all going to have to stay that way." She flicked a quick glance up at me, then down to the sugar again, and changed the subject. "You're looking smart. What's the occasion?"

So there definitely were reasons why there'd been no outward progress between her and Erik? Now I really itched to know what they were.

"It's my day for good works," I said, lifting the Red Cross

bag from beside my ankle where I'd leaned it for safe keeping. "Collecting down Paradise Road."

Heather eased the sugar grains in beside the little vase of flowers on the table. "The long one that runs out to the gun club and the archery building?"

That stopped me in my tracks for a few seconds. Did it? Not being a shooter or an archer I'd never visited either, but I'd definitely glimpsed at least one big building along the far end. Out past civilization where loud noises wouldn't annoy anyone.

It pains me to admit it but I'd been driven most of the way down there by my former husband, Duncan Skeene, when he was only my fiancé. He was hoping for a little action on a blanket under a tree, and I'd been expecting a nice hotel room. Neither of us got what we wanted because there was a surprisingly steady stream of traffic going past for an apparently dead-end road.

I nodded slowly. "I think I know where you mean."

Archery building? Arrows? The arrow in Matthew's back?

Since I'd come across the grisly scene, veterinarian Lisa's youngest son, Pete, had been dancing through my mind and being firmly banished every time he appeared. Pete is twelve. Mad on archery, and apparently quite good at it, but there was no way he'd have stood on that box and shot Matthew Boatman. Maybe there were lots of other local prospects I'd never suspected?

"Erik takes me to the gun club," Heather said, a dreamy expression on her face. "It's... amazing."

I'm sure my eyebrows jumped. "You at the gun club? What for?"

"Why shouldn't I be there? It's an interest of his."

"But... but..." I.sounded like an old car with engine trouble. "What do *you* do there?"

"Shoot guns of course. Target practice." She grinned and shook her head at me. "Merry – don't tell me I've shocked you?"

"Not... really," I managed. Erik and guns kind of went together too easily. Erik and his helicopter. Erik and his ridiculously thorough local knowledge, even though he and John have lived in Drizzle Bay for only a couple of years. American Erik with the shady and never-discussed reputation of being an assassin and a Black Ops specialist?

He's known to everyone as the affable and businesslike co-owner of The Burkeville Bar and Café. And the drop-off pilot for John Bonnington's adventure treks. He also arranges expensive sightseeing flights for cruise-boat passengers, but I discovered some very dodgy files last year in the hidden office at the cottage at the Point. DS Bruce Carver has avoided confirming or denying anything, but there's definitely *something* going on with Erik and the Police – or maybe even at Government level.

"I was hopeless to start with," Heather confessed, distracting me from my speculation. "But once Erik gave me a few pointers I started doing better."

I could easily picture them. Heather looking blonde and fragile and full of trepidation, and Erik, who's a ball of muscle and protective as a bear. I bet he slid an arm around her, snuggled her in against his big chest, and held her steady while she pulled the trigger. Why doesn't anyone snuggle *me* against their chest?

"Rifles or pistols?" I asked, trying to sound as though I knew more than I really did. Also trying not to sound jealous. I added a spoonful of sugar to my flat white and started stirring rather fast.

"Both," she enthused. "But I liked the pistol better. Made me feel like a New York cop."

That was hard to picture. English Heather is a part-time baker and sometime actress. Widowed, close to forty, sister of our vicar, and drama coach for several school productions. Anyone less like a New York cop was hard to imagine. "Maybe with a dark wig and the uniform," I said doubtfully.

"Speaking of which, I have to wear all the gear when I'm there," she added. "The hi-viz vest, the ear-protectors, the safety goggles."

"I should think so!" I had no trouble imagining Erik dressing her up, testing straps for tightness and so on. Maybe letting his hands wander a little while he was at it.

She flashed me a mischievous glance. "I didn't much like aiming at those targets to start with. But once I started doing better, there was no stopping me. Straight through the heart, baby! Erik was quite impressed."

I had to suppose Matthew Boatman had been shot through the heart, although from the back and not the front.

I may have shivered slightly as I asked, "Do the archery people use the same building?"

Heather tilted her head. "Their area's off to one side. Different entrance, but it's through the same gate."

"Amazing the things you don't know about your own little patch of the world," I said as she rose to go back to the kitchen. "Duncan Skeene took me courting down there once. Not as lonely as he'd hoped for." I pointed to the remains of my muffin. "Is this yours or Iona's?"

"Mine. You like it?" Her big blue eyes sparkled.

"Love it! You'll outdo her if you're not careful."

"Not much chance of that." She wiggled her fingers in goodbye as she moved away, looking pleased with my comment.

Which left me alone to sip my coffee and think about poor old Matthew again. I mentally patted myself on the back because I'd now resisted blurting out the shattering news of his death to a whole three people. Iona, Lucy, and Heather.

So Drizzle Bay had an archery club? How many members? No doubt Detectives Carver and Wick would be through that shared gate in no time, sniffing around for evidence. I wished it could be me, but no – I'm only good for cat beds and kibble.

I stared down at my half demolished muffin and picked a bit more off the side. I really should buy another one and take it home for Graham's lunch, but maybe not until I'd got a biggish bag of cat food into the car and worked out what to use by way of plastic sheeting underneath the beds. And how about food and water bowls? Perhaps Iona had containers intended for recycling? I'd ask her once I finished my coffee.

"Merry!" said a familiar voice as Paul McCreagh dropped down into the well-used chair opposite me. "Can you stand my company for a while?"

"Absolutely. I've just been talking to your sister." I pointed to the remains of my chocolate and fig muffin. "Try one of these – Heather's own creation."

He tapped his dog-collar. "I'll be lucky if Iona lets me pay for it, poor impoverished clergyman that I am."

"Vicar," Iona called from behind the nearby counter, right on cue. "A little something to eat?"

He reached into his pocket.

"And don't think you're paying for it," she added. "Tea?"

Paul rolled his eyes at me before turning in her direction. "I really can pay my own way, Iona. You're very generous, but why not treat someone who deserves it more than me?"

Iona twinkled her little birdy eyes at him. "Vicar, you know quite well my daily leftovers go to good homes."

"Indeed they do, but that doesn't mean you need to include me among them."

That set me wondering just where her unsold food ended up. Note to self: ask Paul. In fact there's a lot more I'd like to know about Paul. His father was a British MP. His family home had a big garden. His mother did good works and didn't sound as though she had a job as such. Maybe

Paul was a long way from being the 'impoverished clergy-man' he'd joked about?

I set my coffee down again and turned my mind to the cats. "Iona, if you're in a generous mood could I ask if you have any old empty containers you don't need? Something I can use to hold water?" I decided to stay deliberately vague. If I mentioned cat food she'd get all nosy, knowing I'm more of a dog person.

She bent down and peered at me through the glass of the display cabinet. "Should be some tubs and so on in the recycling bin. See what Heather can find you." Happily she was distracted from wanting to know more by Paul stepping forward to claim his fig and chocolate muffin.

He was back in a few seconds. His tea would follow.

"So where are the 'good homes' her leftovers go to?" I asked.

The corners of his mouth tucked in. Not quite a smile. More of a suggestive tease of one. I sometimes think our vicar is as yummy as Iona's baking.

"My basketball boys have bottomless pits for stomachs," he said.

His basketball boys are giants. Lanky, clumsy, full of testosterone and misguided energy. "And they don't always get the best food at home?"

He breathed in, nodding slowly. "Iona's ham and salad rolls have a lot more nourishment in them than the deep-fried rubbish some of the kids seem to live on."

I watched as concern and regret and pride were reflected

in his dark brown eyes. "And I'll bet there are always exactly enough to go around at practice sessions? She'd make extras, if not?"

His almost-smile became more definite. "Yes, pretty sure that happens."

"She's very generous," I said. "Pretends to be a hard nut to crack, but she has a heart of gold."

Honestly, kill me! I'm a book editor and the best I can manage is a sentence full of old-fashioned clichés...

Paul looked up as Heather arrived with his tea. He has much better manners than I do because he'd waited until his drink arrived before starting on his muffin. Then again, he hadn't been pounding the pavements half the morning and discovering dead bodies in overcrowded kitchens.

"Heather," I said. "Iona says I can have a rummage in your recycling to see about plastic containers that are being thrown out. Okay if I come through to the kitchen in a few minutes?"

She set the tea down. "Heavens yes – the more stuff we can repurpose, the better."

An oven timer buzzed loudly somewhere behind her and she bustled away. The family at the next table rose, gathered up their belongings, and departed. Suddenly Paul and I had more privacy.

"Can I tell you something?" I murmured, keeping half an eye on Iona in case she wanted to know what was going on. When Paul nodded, I said, "Have you met Matthew Boatman from Paradise Road? Old guy, very neat front garden."

"Comes to my Seniors Afternoons," Paul confirmed. "Somewhere else Iona's leftovers are appreciated."

I sank my teeth into my bottom lip. I was bursting to tell someone, and if a clergyman couldn't keep a secret, no-one could, so I added quietly, "I'm afraid he's dead. It's not official yet, so don't spread it around. I've been collecting for the Red Cross this morning and I found him. I'm jinxed."

Paul delayed picking up his muffin and reached for my hand instead. "You're not jinxed. But you're shaking."

"Well, it wasn't nice."

He grimaced. "Had he been dead for a while, Merry?"

I shook my head. "No – maybe only from sometime yesterday. Iona said he came in for date scones on Thursday, as usual."

Paul's face relaxed a little. "So she knows?" he asked.

"No." I cast a quick glance all around the Café. "No," I repeated. "It would be all over the village then. He might have relatives who need to be told first. He was shot in the back with an arrow. In his kitchen."

There was a loud clatter of the cup landing back on Paul's saucer as he reacted to my quiet information. "How the... heck?"

I'm sure he would have said worse in other circumstances.

"Through the window, I think. It's one of those old-fashioned louvre glass ones so it's probably always partly open."

"You called the cops?"

"Yes, of course. They're there now. The place is a total mess inside. He's a hoarder."

Paul squeezed my hand. "Wouldn't have picked that from his tidy garden. Mind you, I've never been inside the house."

"I doubt many people have. And there are cats galore that I've offered to feed on-site."

A boyish grin transformed his face. He looked a lot like a younger Hugh Grant when he smiled. "Cunning plot to be part of the action, Merry?" He released my fingers and glanced around. Yes, it was rather a public place to be holding hands with a parishioner, even if it was meant as friendly consolation after a big fright.

3

GREENHOUSE CATS

I SHRUGGED. "Well, I found him so I'd like to know more. And someone has to look after the poor old pussies. There might be five or six of them."

He lifted his teacup again now I was onto safer topics than arrows in Matthew's back. I couldn't help watching his mouth as it made contact with the rim of the cup and he sipped. He was such a nice man. Friendly, helpful, and handsome. And still apparently in the grip of PTSD from his time as a chaplain in Afghanistan. Heather and I talked about him sometimes. Just as I had hopes for her and Erik, she had hopes for Paul and me, but he'd told me more than once he hasn't beaten it yet, and feels he needs to before he can move on with his life.

I drank some more of my coffee. Would I choose to marry a vicar? Would I even qualify? (Not that I know quite what's expected, but I'm divorced and I don't have a totally innocent past.)

On the other hand there's John Bonnington from The Burkeville Bar and Cafe. He gave me a fake kiss to make Duncan, my slimy ex-husband, jealous just before Christmas. Well I think it was intended to be fake. It turned pretty real pretty fast as far as I was concerned. Heather and Erik practically had to pry us apart. John certainly doesn't have an innocent past. He learned to kiss like that somewhere, and he's Erik's Black Ops buddy if those files were correct.

I gave myself a mental shake; back to the cats.

"So Bruce Carver and Marian Wick will put any cat beds they find out into the front yard, and I'm going to set up a kitty-motel in a little greenhouse there. And call by and feed them when I'm out walking Manual and Daniel."

Paul practically snorted tea everywhere. "Those silly names," he spluttered. "They get me every time."

I grinned. "I know. That's why I didn't say 'Manny and Dan'." I popped the last piece of muffin into my mouth.

"So do they have any idea who did it?" he asked, dropping his volume again and casting a quick glance in Iona's direction.

I shook my head until I swallowed the delicious gooey mouthful and washed it down with the last of my flat white. "I didn't expect there'd be too many people with access to bows and arrows in Drizzle Bay, but your sister tells me there's an archery club."

Paul's eyes opened wider. "How does she know that?"

I was going to enjoy this *so* much...

"Because Erik takes her to the gun club, and the archery people are next door."

Sure enough his jaw dropped and he sat there looking like a gob-smacked goldfish for a couple of seconds. "What does he expect her to do there?" he eventually croaked.

"They shoot at targets. She says she's getting quite good at it."

He shook his head. "Unbelievable. No-one in our family has ever been into the huntin'-shootin'-fishin' lifestyle. Our father was always too busy with his politics, and our mother is into good works and gardening." He narrowed his eyes. "He'd better not be trying to recruit her for anything shady?"

That surprised a laugh out of me. "I'm sure he's not. He seems very... protective of her."

"And he'd better keep it that way," Paul said, taking a big fierce bite out of his muffin.

This effectively put an end to the conversation for a while, so I pointed backward in the general direction of the kitchen and muttered, "Just going to check the recycling for possible cat bowls."

Heather welcomed me in when I poked my head around the doorframe. She had an unflattering elasticated blue hat covering her lovely blonde hair.

"Do I need one of those?" I asked, hoping I didn't.

She shook her head. "Not unless you're anywhere near the ingredients. Can't allow hairs to float into the baking."

"Euw."

"Gotta be done. Recycling's over there." She pointed to two bins in the corner – one for plastics and glass; one for paper-based packaging.

After a short rummage I found several things that might do so I stacked them together, nodded my thanks over the noisy mixer, gave Paul a wave on the way out, and left to put my freebies in the car.

It made sense to go home and change out of my good gear and into jeans and an old oatmeal-colored jersey before I did anything else. Heaven knows how cobwebby the green-house was, or how furry the cat beds might be.

I hadn't yet bought Graham a muffin, but there was no sign of him at home, and no sign of his Mercedes, either, when I checked the garage. I gave him a call. He was some-where windy. I could hear the air blowing past the phone when he answered.

"Where are you?" I asked.

"Burkeville Golf Club. Trying to win back the tenner Maurie Jacobs took off me last time."

Excellent. "Good luck with that. So you won't be home for lunch?"

"No – we'll grab a bite on the way home."

My guilt at not buying him a muffin receded. "Okay – just a quick question: any idea where the big plastic bags are? The ones the new beds came in?"

Graham never throws anything out so I was rewarded with instructions to look on top of the old wardrobe in the back of the garage. When our parents died and we inherited the house, neither of us quite wanted to sleep in their bed so we'd bought a new one apiece and donated theirs to the charity shop. And yes, careful Graham had folded and stacked the bed-bags away 'in case'. In case of what, I've no idea. Probably not in case of waterproofing the floor of a greenhouse so the many cats of a murdered man could stay dry and comfortable.

I peered up. "Yes – I can see them. I'll borrow one if that's all right? Say 'hi' to Maurie for me. Enjoy your game. Hope you win."

One dusty big bed-bag and a jumbo size pack of Fortune Kitty later, I was on my way back to the scene of the crime. Honestly, the things they name cat food! Pussy-Nom-Nom. Kitty-Delish. Delite-a-Cat... Hopefully my lot would be 'delited' with their new accommodation and catering. Equally hopefully, they'd soon relocate themselves elsewhere in the neighborhood.

There were several vehicles now parked in the street outside Matthew's neat little house; DS Carver's boring grey sedan, one brightly checker-board-painted police car, and a big wagon thing that was less than an ambulance but plenty big enough to transport a body. WPC Moody – she of the rather strong calves who'd been first on the scene when Isobel Crombie was murdered in the aisle of St Agatha's Church a few months ago – was on gate duty. Several nosy neighbors wanted to know what had happened and she had her elbows planted on the top of the gate and was deflecting them with comments like, "An official announcement will be made once next-of-kin have been informed."

I couldn't help thinking she'd put fewer cats amongst the pigeons if she just said, "We're investigating a burglary."

Of course it was going to be pretty upsetting for them when they did find out what had happened. I knew some of them to say hello to, and recognized another couple I'd collected from before I got to Matthew's place. Unfortunately for the Red Cross, the turmoil put any further collecting here out of the question for now.

Then Lurline Lawrence from the Drizzle Bay Animal Center hove into view with two large and hairy dogs on leads so I took a few steps back in her direction to have a private word. She raised an eyebrow at my big bag of cat food. "Taking over from me?"

I drew her further out of earshot. "Saving you a job, I hope. There are several cats living here that need feeding. With any luck they'll drift off and find themselves new homes in a few days."

"Not if you keep feeding them here."

I sank my teeth into my bottom lip. "You think I'll make it worse rather than better?"

"Depends how bad it is in the first place," practical Lurline said.

"Bad," I whispered. "Keep it to yourself because it's not official yet, but old Matthew Boatman is dead. Murdered."

Lurline's big eyes became even rounder. "How do you know?" she hissed back.

"I found him."

"Not *another* one, Merry," she groaned, as though I did it on purpose.

"I think I'm jinxed," I muttered. "Three bodies in less than a year. Honestly, this isn't normal. Who else has things like this happen to them?"

Lurline shook her head and her dreadlocks bounced like a collection of long, springy sausages.

I glanced back to WPC Moody. Past her I saw one very large cat bed on the lawn and a couple of smaller ones. Probably the big one was really a dog bed. I eyed the jumbo size bag of Fortune Kitty. It didn't look so big any more. How many animals would I be feeding? "Well, I'm going to give it a go," I told Lurline, hefting the food out of the way of the sensitive noses and whiskery snouts of the dogs she was walking. "If it doesn't work out, I guess it'll become your job."

"Thanks for nothing," she said. "Bruce!" She gave the lead of the taller dog a twitch and he turned his attention from the Fortune Kitty to my crotch.

I lowered the cat food none too gently to bump him out of the way. I didn't need dog-slobber on my jeans or his hot breaths on my hoo-ha. Certainly not from someone with the same name as DS Carver.

"Do you think you'll be able to re-home these two?" I asked. "They're very big, aren't they?"

"But such sweeties," she said, giving the one she'd called Bruce a vigorous scrub around the jaw and ears. Bruce closed his eyes and leaned into her. Just as well Lurline is a solidly-built woman or she'd have had trouble staying upright.

"And what's this one's name?" I put the Fortune Kitty on the ground and stood in front of it to repel intruders.

"Hamburger," she said with a grin. "Or that's what was written on a baggage label around his neck when I found him tied up outside the shelter one morning last week. No registration tags on his collar, so unless someone wants a big dog and is prepared for the expense of registering him and so on, poor Hamburger's days might be numbered."

I looked down into his imploring golden eyes.

No.

Just no.

No room in my life for someone that size, and he'd probably eat Graham's spaniels in two bites. Two spaniels came nowhere near to equaling the weight of one Hamburger.

"What is he – part Irish Wolf-hound, part Great Dane?" I wondered.

"My best guess, too," Lurline agreed. "But back to the other elephant in the room, Merry." She dropped her voice to a murmur. "Matthew's dead. Who did it? How?"

"And why," I added dolefully. "I can't imagine. He was such a nice, inoffensive little man. Wouldn't hurt a fly."

"Or so you'd think," she muttered. "But there's got to be some reason, doesn't there? People don't just – er – shoot? someone else for no reason unless they're total nutters."

"He wasn't shot," I said. "Well, not with a gun."

"Poison darts?" Lurline queried, eyes wide.

I swallowed, and admitted, "Pretty close, actually. A bow and arrow."

"Oh my sainted aunt!"

"Yes, not what you'd expect, but keep it to yourself until they make it official."

"Merry, that's terrible." She pursed her lips and then sucked them practically into her face so she looked like an old lady who'd misplaced her dentures. It was hard not to laugh at her comical expression. Then big hairy Hamburger planted an equally big hairy backside on my left foot and leaned against me.

"He likes you," Lurline said, releasing her lips with a pop.

"He can like me all he wants," I growled. "But I'm very fond of these suede boots and really don't want him sitting on them."

She clicked her tongue and he obediently stood again. "Spoil-sport. Good luck with your cat re-homing project." She dropped her volume and leaned toward me. "Tell me more about the murder when you can."

I wandered back toward the wrought iron gate. WPC Moody remembered me. I wasn't sure if that was good or bad! Or maybe she'd been briefed by Bruce Carver that I might be turning up. I suppose the big bag of Fortune Kitty with its prancing red and blue cats would have been a give-away, too.

She beckoned me through. "Unexpected perp for the flower arranger murdered in the church aisle, eh?" she said chattily.

I guess Drizzle Bay doesn't have that many murders, and in recent times I'd discovered both of them. Or *all* of them now there was a number three. Working as a book editor has made me understandably fussy about grammar.

"Yes, not who anyone thought," I agreed. It certainly hadn't been who *I'd* had in my sights, although it had all happened so fast no one had found a serious prospect among the many gossiped-about possibilities. Drizzle Bay is so small that people know each other, or at least know *of* each other. Many of us knew old Isobel Crombie because of her church work. Beautiful flower arrangements, mostly from blooms grown in her big garden out at The Point. I never expected I'd become temporary caretaker of the place until a home was found for her two little white Bichons. They now belong to our local butcher and his wife, Bernie and Aroha. Not a bad fate for a dog; they were looking quite tubby when I last saw them.

I'd slipped the car keys into my jeans pocket so I had both hands free for the Fortune Kitty. It wasn't far to the greenhouse now so I balanced the bag of food on one too-curvy hip and scooped up a small cat bed from the lawn before making my way around the side of Matthew's old cottage. The path broadened out into a square of concrete beside the garage. You could put an outdoor table and chairs on it, but Matthew hadn't. Then it went back to being a path.

The sliding door was further open than it had been. Maybe a sinewy policeman with a snaky build, or possibly uber-slender Marian Wick had checked out the space? The box in the corner was missing so I assumed someone was thinking along the same lines as me. It was terribly hard not to dash off around the corner of the house and see if they had the box in position...

I bumped the door further aside with an elbow, and the metal made a fearsome squeal as it reluctantly scraped far enough to let me in. I set the Fortune Kitty and the small cat bed on the flower pot shelf and scurried back to the car for the big plastic bag.

"Going okay with the cats?" WPC Moody asked as she opened the gate to let me out.

I nodded. "He seems to have quite a lot of them."

"And quite a lot of everything else, too," she agreed, closing the gate and sending me a terrible impersonation of a wink-wink nudge-nudge stand-up comedian to indicate she knew something she wasn't prepared to share with the lingering neighbors.

"Have you seen inside?" I asked. The neighbors leaned closer, hoping for any shred of gossip.

"No," WPC Moody said. "DC Wick told me." She followed this with a big sigh and a rosy blush.

Oh wow – did I detect amorous feelings toward pretty Marian Wick? I suspected poor WPC Moody was up against hunky John Bonnington from The Burkeville Bar, and I knew which one I'd choose if I was Marian Wick! But maybe I was wrong? I raised an enquiring eyebrow and sent her a slight grin. That caused the blush to deepen. No, I wasn't wrong.

"Mr Boatman had a lot of belongings," I agreed. And then thought my past tense might have given the game away to anyone listening.

However, right at that moment a noisy motorcycle coasted up and braked to a flashy stop. A jeans-and-black-jacketed figure slid off, kicked the stand into place with a hefty black boot, and strode across the road. "How is he?" the rider demanded, hauling off her helmet and releasing a cascade of bright red hair. "I'm Jude Boatman."

4

THE PRODIGAL DAUGHTER-IN-LAW

"YOU'RE HIS *DAUGHTER?*" WPC Moody squawked as I returned from the car with the huge plastic bag.

"Daughter-in-law." Which was snapped in a cut-crystal voice.

WPC Moody's muscular bulk lurched back a little, but she didn't let go of the gate. "What have you heard?"

"That cops are swarming all over the house. The village is full of it."

Was it? It seemed unlikely to me. I'd only told Paul and Lurline.

"Well, an official announcement will be made once the next of kin have been informed," WPC Moody said.

"Don't be ridiculous. I *AM* the next of kin," the Jude person snapped, peeling off her gloves and thrusting her arm though the chin strap of her crash helmet so it hung from her elbow. "Let me by." She sounded like an old-fashioned nobleman demanding a highwayman get out of her way.

"As you can see," WPC Moody explained through gritted teeth, "The Police are not 'swarming'. We don't swarm. But there has been an incident which requires investigation. Members of the public will only contaminate the crime scene. Please step back."

Auburn-haired Jude tossed her considerable mane of hair and I had to take a step aside to avoid being hit in the face with it.

"Oi!" I said. Hardly ladylike, but I had no hands free to defend myself because they were clutching the big plastic bed-bag.

WPC Moody unlatched the wrought iron gate and both Jude Boatman and I dived for the gap just as DS Bruce Carver appeared at the front door. I fended Jude off with my unwieldy armful and squeezed through. I did, after all, have permission to be there.

"Hey!" she objected as Moody somehow got the gate closed again. Then, sensing DS Carver might be in charge of things she pasted on a smile and called, "Hello? I need to know how Pa-in-law is."

I took my time sorting through the selection of remaining cat beds so I could eavesdrop. I was only a few feet away.

"And you are?" Bruce Carver asked, standing a little straighter.

"Jude Boatman. Someone told me there'd been trouble."

I put the bed-bag down and wasted some time by refolding it, listening intently over the crackles the plastic made.

Instead of succumbing to the redhead's confidence and charm, he barked, "And where did you hear that?"

She fluffed up her hair with her free hand. It was the curly kind which seemed to recover pretty well from being squashed inside the crash helmet. "In the village. Someone said the police were here."

Entirely possible I suppose, although there hadn't been much traffic driving past, and a single squad car hardly indicated any great emergency. Then again, thinking back to how many people had whipped out their phones and photographed the half-closed garage door at home when the leg of beef was discovered in Graham's Merc last Christmas, maybe there'd been some neighborly gossiping and tweeting going on? Perhaps with shots of WPC Moody in her dark uniform guarding the gate like an aggressive pit-bull?

"This is an active crime scene right now, Ms Boatman," the DS announced. "Maybe we could have a private word in my car?" He waved an arm toward his grey sedan and paced across toward the gate.

"But what's actually *happened*?" an old chap in a Fair Isle jumper called out. "He's a good neighbor. Is he all right?"

"An official announcement will be made once the next of kin have been informed," Bruce Carver said.

"I *AM* the next of kin," Jude Boatman bellowed, digging into one of the many pockets in her jacket and producing a slim wallet. She extracted her driver's license with its photo

I.D., leaned over the gate, and waved it under his nose. "His only sister and his only son are dead, so that leaves *me*. If something's happened to Matthew, tell me now and then maybe these vultures will go away."

She glared at the collection of neighbors who'd recently been joined by the Coastal Courier's owner and sometime reporter, Bob Burgess. There were muttered objections to her description but no-one backed off an inch.

"Your choice," DS Carver said, shrugging as he inspected her photo. "This is most irregular, and there's been no official identification, but I can confirm that Mr Boatman is deceased. We have a great deal of work to do yet so I'll thank you all to leave us in peace to do it."

A chorus of gasps and exclamations ensued. Crouched on the lawn I had a really good view of Jude Boatman as she let go of her hair, clutched her crash helmet in both hands, and looked as though she was going to be sick into it. I hoped she wasn't because she'd parked her gloves in there.

"How did he die?" someone demanded. Probably Bob from the Courier.

"He was shot through his kitchen window," DS Carver conceded.

"An execution-style killing?" a woman demanded.

"Don't be ridiculous, Dawn," Mr Fair Isle said. "Who'd want to execute Matthew? They'd have to do it through our hedge."

"So *we* could have been killed instead?"

"Chance would be a fine thing," someone muttered. Not her husband, I hoped.

DS Carver fixed the small crowd with his piercing gaze. "No further announcements will be made today. Can you please disperse and let us get on with our investigation."

"I'm coming in," Jude Boatman declared.

The DS aimed an even colder glare at her. "You're certainly not. No-one's coming in without my say-so."

Ms denim-and-leather pointed to me and demanded, "What's *she* doing in there, then?"

It probably wasn't my business, but I dived in with, "Taking care of the cats until they can be re-homed."

She sniffed. "Beastly animals."

"Would anyone like a new cat?" I yelled hopefully.

Bruce Carver's declaration hadn't got the crowd moving, but that did! Obviously no-one wanted a cat so the poor old pussies would need to display their charms further afield if they expected anyone to take them in.

As the neighbors drifted away, their comments and speculations floated back on the sea breeze.

Bob Burgess attempted to grill WPC Moody over the gate but she sensibly said little more than Bruce Carver had already revealed; that Matthew Boatman was dead and had been shot through his kitchen window 'some hours ago'. She must have invented that piece because the bird's head and the smelly can of cat food had me thinking 'yesterday' rather than 'some hours ago'.

Jude Boatman dug into her wallet again and produced a

business card that she handed to WPC Moody with a sneer. "Tell him to get in touch when he finds the time. I'm not hanging around here until he's ready to talk sense."

She stomped away, buckles jingling, and I heard the motorcycle start with a thunderous roar. A few seconds later it shot off down Paradise Road.

"What does she do?" Bob Burgess asked, trying to get a glimpse of the card.

Moody tilted it in the sun. "Gold letters," she said. "Hard to read." She squinted. "Gemologist. What's a gemologist? One of those, anyway. And a bespoke jeweler." Recognition arrived, and her eyebrows rose. "Oh – gemstones!"

Bob Burgess nodded. "She's not in business anywhere around here. I contact everyone in the district offering advertising in the Coastal Courier several times a year. Can I have her info?"

For some reason WPC Moody saw no problem with that, so Bob tapped it into his phone. "You been in the force long?" I heard him ask. Good grief – was he going to interview her? Oh well – maybe a nice public relations piece if she was lucky. Hopefully not speculation about poor Matthew's murder. I cleared my throat as a warning to her to keep being discreet as I gathered up the plastic bag and the biggest cat bed and hauled them around to the greenhouse. Not that it was any of my business!

The little brown and white cat I'd nicknamed Peanut bounded out from among the dead tomato plants as I approached with my big armful. Maybe it had already scented the cat bed or the Fortune Kitty?

"Hi there, Peanut. Checking things out?" I enquired idiotically. It was a pretty animal with stripes and fluffy ruffles around its body. Not big. Female, I decided.

I got a high-pitched 'meow' in return, which made me wonder if it was Peanut who'd jumped down from the newspaper stack inside Matthew's front door. "So where are your friends?" I asked, mentally cringing at my inane question.

I dropped my load on the lawn and regarded the size of the greenhouse versus the size of the plastic bed-bag. Those dried-up old tomato plants definitely had to go, although the flourishing lettuces were right at one end and therefore safe. Pleased I'd changed into jeans, I had a vigorous wrestling match with the tomatoes and their stakes and threw them out on the lawn. Peanut sat and watched, but whizzed off once I started dragging the noisy bag inside. I spread it out, patted it down, anchored it with the large and small cat beds, then returned for the final two.

Well, there wasn't another greenhouse like it anywhere in Drizzle Bay – that was for sure. Maybe not in the whole of New Zealand. I went out to the car one last time and found Bob Burgess and WPC Moody both leaning on the gate, intent on the screen of his phone. "Yes, got her," he said. "From Rotorua. I wonder what she's doing down here?"

"On a road trip?" Moody suggested.

"No luggage."

"Mmmm. Staying in a motel?"

They moved aside to let me through, and I returned almost immediately with the plastic containers I'd uplifted from Iona's recycling to overhear Moody saying, "Not a Kiwi. English? Fancy accent."

Bob shook his head. "A hint of South Africa in it, I thought."

"Really?" Moody asked, nodding hers.

I left them speculating, and looked around for a garden tap so I could get the cats some water. Two of Iona's plastic pails had contained Caramel Glaze and Blueberry Filling according to their labels. I gave each a cautious sniff but whoever had washed them had done a good job. I filled them both to the brim and realized my mistake when I started to slop the chilly contents down my jeans as I made my way back across the lawn. Boy, that was cold! Thinking ahead, I tipped a bit more out and set them just inside the door; no point in dripping water all over the cat beds as well. I upended several of the heavier brick flower pots and braced the pails upright with them. Job done!

But what about the Fortune Kitty? There'd be fighting if several cats all tried to eat together out of a pail. I sidled between the cat beds and checked the pot-shelf again. A wide terracotta saucer, obviously once the drip-catcher for a big pot, lurked near the back. I brushed the cobwebs off it. The moment I ripped the top tab open and started sprinkling the crunchy kibble out, Peanut rushed from under the shrubs by the fence. A bigger, patchy gray cat bounded close behind. As it was many shades of gray I decided he'd be Fifty. They fell to eating as though they hadn't seen food for weeks instead of only one day. Mind you, one day would be plenty long enough for me to miss my meals.

"Hello. How are you going here?" I heard a few minutes later. It was WPC Moody.

I must have looked surprised because she quickly followed up with, "It's okay – the spies have all gone for now. I'd like a cat please."

Knock me down with a feather!

"That's wonderful," I exclaimed. It was the last thing I'd expected. "Do you want to wait until they all turn up before you choose? There are these two, which I've nicknamed Peanut and Fifty, but I reckon there are at least three more." I did a mental count of the possible bed spaces. "Maybe even four? One looked rather Siamese, but they dashed out of the house like rockets. It was hard to tell how many."

WPC Moody sidled a little closer to the greenhouse. Fifty and Peanut took no notice of her. "Poor things," she said. "So hungry."

"One of them almost knocked Bruce Carver over," I added. "Have you seen inside now all the neighbors have gone?"

She bent and touched the tip of Peanut's tail. It was swiftly swished sideways. "No. But DC Wick let slip he had a huge amount of stuff. A fire risk, she said."

"More than that – he's a total hoarder. Maybe keep that to yourself until you're supposed to know about it, but the amount of newspaper stacked in the hallway would have the house up in flames after just one spark."

Moody chewed her bottom lip for a moment. "So *that's* what she meant. Do you think he was killed because of it? Seems odd, to say the least."

I smirked. "Not killed for all the old newspapers. But who knows what else is in there? Honestly, the doors are impossible to get through. All the hallway rooms are barricaded off. And you can't see through from the outside because the curtains are closed."

Her gaze assumed a suspicious glint. "So how did *you* get in?" She reached down to stroke Fifty. He looked up, round-eyed, and resumed eating as I repeated the 'collecting for the Red Cross/door left open' scenario.

"Huh. Way to start a nice Saturday." She gave Fifty another stroke. "The grey one likes me better," she said, just as the lanky Siamese-lookalike rushed past us and straight to the terracotta saucer with a hoarse growl. The kibble was disappearing at an alarming rate.

I tried touching Peanut, got a growl as well as a tail-swish, and pulled my hand away. "Nothing makes sense. Matthew was a nice little man. Kind to his cats. Went to Vicar Paul's Seniors Afternoons at Saint Agatha's. Bought two date scones from Iona every Thursday morning. Does that sound like he's in line to be murdered?"

Moody shook her head. "Sounds like you're playing detective again." But it was said without rancor. "Isn't that one *gorgeous*," she added, staring with undiluted longing at the possibly-not-purebred cream and chocolate feline. "I always wanted a cat," she added. "My Dad was allergic, so no chance at home. Or at Police College, of course. Difficult with flatmates, and with the likelihood of being transferred to another town..."

"But surely that might still happen?"

She leaned over and ran a cautious finger along the knobbly spine of the Siamese. "No – I've found my level. Happy with what I'm doing. I bought a little two-bedroom place and I have someone sharing to help out with the mortgage."

I sent her a smile. "Good for you. My brother and I were lucky and inherited our parents' home." I shrugged and dropped my gaze from hers. "Or unlucky. It was at the cost of their lives, unfortunately."

She screwed up her face in sympathy. "About three years ago, wasn't it? I remember that awful accident on the main road."

For some reason I added, "Graham hasn't married and I'm divorced. There's a big yard for his two spaniels, and we rub along okay."

"Mmm... good arrangement." But her attention was back on the cats again. As the Siamese hadn't objected to her first tentative touch, she ran her hand along his back and he arched up against it.

I couldn't help thinking they made an unlikely pair. The cat was bonily elegant and Moody was... I tried to find a better word than chunky, but nothing arrived. I'd based that mostly on her muscular calves, but looking more closely I saw her uniform strained around a boxy body with impressive breasts. She was no way slim like Marian Wick. Probably strong as an ox, though, if she could pass her annual fitness reviews.

"Bess," she said, deserting the cat and thrusting her hand in my direction for a bone-crunching shake. "Bess Moody. I'll love him to bits if he'll have me. He's letting me stroke him, so maybe?"

I glanced at my watch. The afternoon was sliding by. "You don't want to wait for the other cats to turn up? You might like one of them better?"

She released my hand. "I like that one. I'll call him Siam. Male, you reckon?"

I wasn't up for inspecting the nether regions of hungry moggies so I suggested, "From his size, yes. But probably neutered because there don't seem to be any kittens around."

"Wrong time of year for them," Bess Moody said. "They're Christmas, mostly. Even though I've never had a cat, I know a bit."

I nodded along as though I knew a bit too. "You'll need a carry-cage. Maybe Lurline could loan you one from the Animal Shelter to be going on with?"

She smiled. "Good idea. Don't let anyone else have him, will you? I'd better get back to the gate, although I think the nosy parkers are gone now the DS has announced the death. I'll try phoning her from there." She strode away, whistling happily. The march from 'The Bridge on the River Kwai', if I wasn't mistaken. Surely that was Burma, not Siam? When did Siam become Thailand? Must look it up.

I sprinkled some more Fortune Kitty into the big plant saucer and drizzled a little across the lawn to guide the rest of the tribe in, pulled the door almost closed, and wedged a brick in place to hold it from entirely shutting so no-one was either trapped inside or cut off from the food and beds. All done for now.

But finding Matthew? A third body? Why me? I shuddered as the shock finally set in. I needed to get home, have a sit-down with a hot drink, and maybe phone my bestie Steff if the time difference between here and Montreal worked out. I glanced at my watch. About 9.30 where she was. Saturday for me, but still Friday for her.

I heaved the bag of Fortune Kitty into my arms again and carried it toward the car. If I left it on the shelf one of those cats would probably leap up, nudge it over, and tip kibble from here to kingdom come.

Halfway to the gate my phone rang. I fumbled under my big winter jersey to dig it out from my jeans pocket. No – jeans were tighter than remembered... Grimacing, I dumped the bag of food on the lawn, extricated my phone, and glanced at the caller's name before answering.

It was Paul. That's Vicar Paul McCreagh to you.

"Paul," I said, trying not to sound too thrilled. It was a serious day, after all.

"Merry."

I heard the smile in his voice. I won't say my heart beats

faster when it's his voice (English, BBC-ish, could listen for ages) but I'm always pleased.

He cleared his throat. "I'm assuming you're feeling less than fantastic after finding number three, so how about I take you out for a meal at The Burkeville?"

I noticed he didn't say 'body' or 'murder'. Just 'number three'. He's so kind.

"To cheer me up?"

"If that's what you need. Are you doing okay?"

I think I sighed, and he immediately picked up on it because he added, "We don't have to. Just thought you might like company."

"I'm not going to mention the arrow," I grumped. "You know they'll all ask questions."

"Probably," he conceded after a couple of seconds. "Maybe not such a brilliant idea, then?"

I scrambled to make amends for my lack of enthusiasm. "No – it's a lovely idea, Paul. Thank you. I was planning to call in to Lisa's next. I haven't seen her for a while, and I'm hoping she's there because I want to talk to one of the kids."

I heard speculation creep into his voice as he asked, "Are you up with her latest news?"

If human ears could prick up, mine did. "*What* news? What's been happening?"

He gave a quiet chuckle. "If you haven't heard, then I'm not going to spoil her big reveal."

5

GOING UP

"*Pawwwwlll!*" I exclaimed, no doubt sounding like a petulant child.

He outright laughed this time. "Nope – it's her story to tell. I'll pick you up at seven?"

Well, if he was going to keep secrets from me, I wouldn't be telling him the real reason I planned to visit veterinarian Lisa Smedley. "Lovely. Thank you," I said, less than graciously. I disconnected, pushed the phone back into my pocket, and heaved the bag of Fortune Kitty into my arms again.

Lisa's youngest son is mad on archery and I'd been thinking 'murder... arrow... local knowledge...' and hoping twelve-year-old Pete could tell me more than Heather had. She'd mentioned the Archery Club and Gun Club shared the same gate at the end of Paradise Road. Better than nothing if

I managed a chat with him – it would help me sound as though I knew a small amount, anyway.

Paul and Lurline were the only people I'd told about Matthew Boatman's grisly death. I'd noted DS Bruce Carver provided no details except 'shot' to the crowd outside the gate and thought I'd better tread carefully and keep it that way from now on. But what was Lisa's big news?

It took only a few minutes to drive down Drizzle Bay Road to the vet clinic. Whoa – what was going on? A white Halliday Construction van departed as I arrived and piles of timber and a rusty red shipping container filled one corner of the parking area. Was she extending the premises? Maybe taking on staff? She always seemed busy. As a single mum with three teenagers and a serious job, she could certainly do with more help.

Then, as I slid out of my car I almost tripped over with surprise. Barreling out of the front doorway, and carrying a long plank on one substantial shoulder, was her estranged husband, Ten Ton.

Maybe estranged no longer? He certainly looked at home and without a care in the world. Was this what Paul had meant by 'her latest news'?

I clutched the top of my car door for a few seconds, absorbing Ten's Halloween-pumpkin grin and his huge muscled frame. At six-foot-seven he's a foot and a half taller than little Lisa. I try not to imagine them 'together', but they're so physically mismatched that my naughty brain sends me pictures.

"Ten!" I exclaimed, genuinely happy to see him. "What are you doing here?"

I'm more used to him as the owner/mechanic of the Drizzle Bay auto repair place, although there was that memorable day back in January when I discovered he was a helicopter pilot. He and Erik had flown us out over the countryside to Devon Downs in an effort to find Beefy Haldane and Roddy Whitebottom. Ten is ex-Air Force. I shouldn't have been so surprised.

He thumped the plank down onto a couple of sawhorses and turned to me. Shoulders, chest, arms – all huge in a tight and somewhat holey grey jumper. Waist and hips surprisingly trim in well-worn jeans. Legs long enough so he probably didn't need a ladder to reach ceilings. My mother would have described him as 'a fine figure of a man'.

"We're extending upward," he said, jerking his chin at the vet clinic's roof. If I was as tall as him I could possibly have seen what he meant.

"So you're back together?"

He nodded enthusiastically. "Yeah – got past the rubbish and she saw common sense."

Well, maybe. I was willing to bet Lisa would describe it differently. Namely that Ten was the one who'd seen common sense, but whatever...

"I'm really pleased," I said. "It hurt to see you apart. Is she home?"

"Showering off farm dirt, last I saw her." He waggled his eyebrows and grinned. He looked so happy at the prospect.

"Somewhere inside for sure," he added, trying to look less lascivious.

I nodded my thanks and walked in. I hadn't known Lisa lived behind the clinic until I'd spotted sheets on the clothes-line from a helicopter flight with Erik six months earlier. I'd not expected anyone lived there because it sat amongst a group of commercial premises – an agricultural tanks and plumbing supplies depot, a small-time blueberry processor (sauces, preserves, etc.) and several other buildings that weren't prominently sign written. I know one makes kitchen counter tops for a much larger place near Wellington.

Lisa showering off cow dung and mud was ideal because that meant I might find Pete alone. Mac was probably out playing rugby, and I knew Bailey had been collecting for the Red Cross. I'd bet anything she'd be off somewhere with friends the minute she'd handed in her money, swapping her plastic collection bag for chocolate milkshakes and rasp-berry donuts from Iona.

I walked in over drop-sheets laid to protect the floor, and followed my ears to the kitchen. It's much more a staff lunch-room than a true kitchen but Lisa makes it work.

Sure enough, Pete was home. He's small for twelve – takes after Lisa more than Ten, but maybe he'll shoot up in a year or three. He had a noisy techno-beat thing thumping away, and was sitting at the table painting long thin pieces of timber with a small brush. Good opening opportunity!

"Hi Pete. Making arrows?"

He turned down the volume on his iPad and then looked

at me with his father's brown eyes. "Yeah," he said. "But if I had a crossbow, they'd be called bolts."

Huh! A bolt from the blue in Matthew Boatman's case.

"But you don't have a crossbow?"

He shook his head, and his floppy blond hair lifted and settled. The yearning expression on his face told me he'd love one.

"School colors?" I asked as he sighed and resumed painting. I took the sigh as regret for the lack of a crossbow and not because of my interruption.

He became a real study in concentration, tip of his tongue between his teeth for a few seconds as he completed another careful green ring around the blue background. "Yeah – for some of the little kids to try," he said as he finished it, set the brush to rinse, and gave me his full attention.

He's a nice boy. Still just young enough not to be a terrible teenager.

I inspected the other things strewn about the table top. "I didn't know you could make your own. You glue the points on somehow, do you?"

"Arrowheads," he said. "Or nocks. They're not called points. I'll show you."

Nocked Matthew out for sure.

Stop it Merry!

Seconds later Pete turned his screen in my direction to display a website with a heavily bearded man at the top and assorted archery items in columns. "These are just for kids," he said, pointing to timber arrows. "And some are carbon fiber or fiberglass." He indicated evil-looking black ones. "Or there are aluminum shafts, like these golds."

"Do they have silver?" I asked, remembering the metallic flash I'd seen protruding through the chair slats that morning.

Pete scrolled further, then tapped to the next page. "There are these Axis Focused Energy shafts?" he suggested, tilting the screen again so I could see them.

I nodded slowly. In reality I'd got such a quick look I couldn't tell you if Matthew had been shot with painted timber or aluminum or indeed stainless steel, if such things existed. Then I caught sight of something weird. "Wait – is that a bow that folds in half?"

Pete gnawed on his bottom lip. "One of those would be easy on my bike. Then no-one would have to give me a ride."

"True," I murmured, noting the price. Goodness.

I couldn't help thinking the folding version would be a lot easier to skulk around suburbia with, too. No-one would expect a bag that shape to contain anything so deadly.

The whole website was full of lethal-looking weapons when I peered more closely. As lethal-looking as the bearded man in the top banner. I really wouldn't want to come across him on a dark night, especially if he was aiming anything so deadly at me.

I heard the water turn off in the bathroom and grabbed my opportunity. "I never knew there was so much to it, Pete.

Do you belong to the Archery Club down the end of Paradise Road? The one by the Gun Club?"

He killed the website. "Yeah. I'm the youngest by far."

"I have a friend who goes there for pistol practice. I can't imagine doing that, but she enjoys it."

He scrunched up his face. "Don't like guns. Not after we got shot at flying out of Devon Downs with Dad."

Understandable. We'd all been lucky to escape with our lives that day. It had certainly set Paul back in the PTSD department.

"Archery is totally human-powered," I agreed, just as Ten ducked his head under the kitchen doorframe.

"All okay?" he asked.

I looked up, and up, and nodded. "Yes – just discussing arrows with Pete."

"Ah – he has plenty to say about those," Ten agreed. "Don't you Buddy?"

Pete pulled a face, and we were saved from his opinion by Lisa trotting in, securing the sash of a fuzzy violet robe around her waist.

"I thought I heard a female voice," she said. "I knew Bailey was still out with Ebony – and believe me, they'd make a lot more noise than you. Anyone for a cuppa?" She squeezed around behind Pete in the compact kitchen and turned on the tap to fill the electric kettle.

I waggled a finger back and forth between Ten and Lisa. "Very pleased to find you're back together. I bet the kids are thrilled?"

"It's good I won't have to sleep in those bunks with Mac for much longer," Pete inserted morosely.

"There's not all that much room above the auto repair depot, I agree," Ten said, laying a hand on Pete's shoulder. "But we made it work for weekends and holidays, didn't we Bud?"

Lisa cleared her throat with an ominous note, and I dived in first. "So what are you building here?"

Ten drew a deep breath. "Going up in the world," he said. "We don't want the kids crammed in any longer, although the rooms served their purpose until we got things sorted."

"Barely," Lisa sniped. "Earl Grey or Mango? Or peppermint?" She pointed to the jars of tea-bags stacked on a shelf above the counter.

"Mango sounds nice," I said.

She finally smiled. "Go up with Ten and see what's happening while I make it. You look safe for climbing a ladder in those jeans."

Ten ducked under the doorframe again and disappeared.

"I have a story for you later," I said, in a tone that told her it wasn't for her son.

"I'll get dressed and join you. You want some Milo, Pete?"

He looked up from his arrow-painting. "Got anything to eat?"

"The boy with hollow legs," she murmured, reaching out to pat his shoulder and then thinking better of it as he picked up his paintbrush again. "I'll see."

I followed Ten Ton along the trail of drop-sheets and saw

his long legs disappearing against the sky. He hadn't been joking about 'going up in the world'." There was a sizeable hole in the ceiling, and I gripped the ladder rungs and climbed carefully after him. Through the ceiling and then through the actual roof space until we'd skirted a big tarpaulin and were standing on the flattish area over the back portion of the vet clinic.

The view was amazing. Far to the south, and behind me when I swiveled, I saw the brilliant glitter of snow on mountains under the cloudless sky.

"Seaward Kaikouras," Ten said, pointing to the nearer southern range. "And the Inland Kaikouras. It'd be spectacular driving past those right now. Lisa and I took the kids down to Queenstown a few years ago." He pulled a face, the corners of his mouth tightening. "Probably what started the rot – all those hours in the car with five of us constantly sniping at each other. Behind us now, with any luck, but that part of the trip was great."

"Sounds like it," I agreed, quickly adding, "Doesn't Drizzle Bay look amazing from up here?"

At the end of Drizzle Bay Road, Lord Drizzle's farm was verdant green in early spring. The big farmhouse was tucked behind trees, but they were bare of leaves right now and I could see through the branches to the house and barns and other farm buildings. It seemed too close – until I remembered we were already part-way there.

It was all too easy to recall the body on the big X-shaped tree we'd found six months earlier. Drizzle Farm's manager,

Denny McKenzie, had blown the weathered white trunk to smithereens to stop stickybeaks and morbid gawpers from trying to find it on the beach once the Police had finished their work there. Good job, too – no-one needed a reminder of things like that – especially me.

Ten stood quietly as my gaze traveled over the sweep of empty coastline before the streets of the village took over from the countryside. He was a big comforting presence and I was grateful to have him there because the next most obvious landmark was Saint Agatha's church – easy to spot with its steeple pointing to heaven. The memory of finding poor old Isobel Crombie lying dead in the aisle surrounded by the flowers she'd come to arrange was never far from my mind. You don't forget the first body you see. Or the second. And now, horribly, I had a third to think about.

"The rooms under here were only stage one of our initial project," Ten said, hearing the ladder creaking as Lisa climbed. She popped her blonde curls through the hole and up into the sun. He reached out a hand to her, and I noticed he didn't let it go once she was on the roof with us. Then he put an unexpected arm around me, dropped a kiss on Lisa's hair, and said, "Don't go close to the edges, ladies. We need to get some scaffolding up yet."

My heart did a little pitter-pat, even though he was only a borrowed husband. I wouldn't mind having a real one again.

I tried to squash that thought and turned back to the view. Drizzle Bay's main shopping street is wider than the others – the only one with buildings higher than a single floor. Graham's legal office was there somewhere – the office that had been our dad's until his untimely death.

There was a big surf running. Rolling all the way up from the southern ocean. A few dots of black indicated surfers in wetsuits. They were welcome to the chilly experience. I wondered idly – okay, a little more than idly – if one of them was handsome, lanky John Bonnington. Maybe not on a busy Saturday, but if I saw him tonight when I was there with Paul, I might ask.

I shook myself back to the current situation. "So what are you planning to build up here?"

Ten slid his arm away from my shoulders. "Making use of the views," he said.

"Starting with a proper kitchen," Lisa added. "Open-plan into a huge dining and sitting area up here in the sunshine." She turned her head as something caught her attention. "Look – someone's getting a super-size dumpster."

The edge of the big yellow bin flashed in the brilliant light as it was unloaded from the truck. Paradise Road, for sure. The Police were wasting no time getting onto Matthew's clean-up.

"Mmmm, "I said. "That's the story I came to tell you. And with the children out of earshot, now's the ideal time. I – um – do either of you know Matthew Boatman?"

"Six cats," Lisa contributed.

OMG – six! Really?

"He's had a couple of classy little Alfas as long as I've

known him." Ten said. "'64 Guilias – 1600 Sprint Speciales. Heck of a car."

I drew a deep breath. "I'm afraid that dumpster's being dropped off at his place so the police can start a massive clean-up. He's dead – yesterday, they think. And he's a hoarder. The house is absolutely crammed with stuff."

"How on earth do you know that?" Lisa demanded. Then I watched as speculation lit her eyes and transformed her face. "No, Merry! You haven't been digging around again?"

I mashed my lips together in a glum expression. "Not digging in the least. I was collecting for the Red Cross and his front door was slightly open. So I called out when he didn't answer my knocking."

Ten returned his arm to my shoulder and I leaned into him gratefully. "It's a mercy it wasn't Bailey who was doing Paradise Road," I added. Bailey is a fantastic tennis player but she's a very 'girly' girl, and maybe not terribly mature for fourteen or whatever she is now.

Lisa nodded agreement. "Thank goodness." Then she raised her eyebrows encouragingly. I noticed she'd also cuddled closer to Ten. For comfort, or did she regard me as competition? No, surely not...

"I doubt she'd have done what I did," I said. "I pushed the door open, still calling out his name, and went a few steps along the hallway. He's not young. He lives alone so I was somewhat concerned. I found him sitting dead in the kitchen."

"Natural causes, then," Ten said.

I shook my head, and a big shudder worked its way down my body. "He'd been shot," I whispered, managing not to mention the arrow.

"Oh my sainted aunt!" Lisa exclaimed. "But you're okay?"

"Yes, I'm fine. A bit shaky now and again, as you can see." I somehow managed a smile for her. "So you didn't know? You haven't had the radio on? Or seen it on your phones' newsfeeds? I'm sure they'll have made it public by now because Bruce Carver confirmed it at the house when Matthew's daughter-in-law turned up and got stroppy."

Ten shook his head. "I've been up and down that ladder for the last couple of hours giving Lee Halliday a hand. He's doing the real work."

Lisa shrugged. "And I've been out at the new-look Devon Downs which is being rebranded as Lucky Golden Empire, if you please. Then to Betty McGyver's Horse Heaven in Old Bay Road to check out a very pretty new foal. Come and we'll have that tea. Ten can tell you how we're rearranging the rooms downstairs so everyone gets their own bedroom, and you can tell us the rest of Matthew's story."

Ten climbed down first, being most used to the ladder. I went next because little Lisa jokingly said it was better he caught me if I missed my step because I'd smash her to bits if she tried to. Not very flattering, but true. She came last, and then bustled ahead of us to the kitchen.

Pete looked up with an air of resignation. "You want the table?"

"No sweetie," Lisa said. "We'll take our cuppas to the living room."

"Okay," he said. "So when's dinner?"

Lisa checked her watch. "In two and a half hours."

"But I'm *hungry*."

"You're always hungry," she said, producing a cake tin from a cupboard and peering inside it. "There you go – knock yourself out before the others get home." She set it on the table with a knife.

"So what are *we* eating?" Ten asked.

She raised an eyebrow. "You've finished growing. You had lunch. You can wait for dinner."

"Working like a slave here," he grumbled, but it was good-natured. He indicated I should precede him into the room they used for watching TV, and we sat on the big fawn velour sectional that took up two walls.

Lisa appeared soon after, holding a tray loaded with three mugs, three plates, and a creased brown paper bag. She set it on the coffee table. "Mango," she said, pushing a mug toward me. She handed one to Ten and kept the third for herself. "Baking by Betty McGyver." She opened the bag. "She gave me a fresh muffin for each of the kids. Carrot and sultana. Pete will be fine with the remains of that chocolate cake, Bailey will have gone to Iona's with Ebony for sure, and I'll lay odds Mac and his team-mates will be stuffing themselves with burgers as soon as their rugby's over. These are all ours." She tucked her legs up and snuggled into Ten. "So why would anyone want to shoot old Matthew?"

6

POSSIBILITIES

"MAYBE THEY WERE AFTER HIS CARS," Ten said. "The '64 Alfa Guilia Sprint Speciale is a classic, and worth at least a hundred and fifty thou Kiwi bucks. He's had them since new, and they're still in amazing nick. Always garaged."

I reached for a muffin. "No, surely not. You don't murder someone for a car."

Lisa blew on her tea. "He had more than one? That's weird. He never seemed to go anywhere much."

Ten took a sip, pulled a face, and set his mug down again. "One used to be his wife's. Crikey that's hot."

"Eat your muffin then," Lisa said, as though she was his mother. I privately thought she could moderate her tone, but at least she was cuddled up against him and looking affectionate. Maybe they'd be okay together this time?

I watched as the corners of Ten's mouth twitched and concluded he was trying not to react to her bossiness.

"You'd murder for *some* cars," he said. "If you thought you could get away with it. A '56 Aston Martin DBR1 went for $22 million at Southebys in 2017."

Lisa and I turned disbelieving eyes on him.

"Scarce, famous, great condition," he added. "Only five of them ever made – not that old Matthew had one of those tucked away." He bit into his muffin.

"It's a long, narrow garage," I said, trying to picture it. "Maybe two cars end-to-end if he still has them both?"

"His wife was called Emma, I think," Lisa mused. "Or maybe Emily? He sometimes mentioned her when he brought the cats in for vaccinations and so on, but I know he was widowed ages back."

"Years and years," I agreed. "So long ago I can't even remember how she died." I took a sip of tea. "It's anyone's guess what he had crammed into that house. I wasn't joking when I said he was a hoarder. The kitchen's pretty disgusting, and I've no idea what's in all the rooms off the hallway because that's totally stacked with old newspapers and magazines. Feet high. You can't get the doors open to see."

"Not surprised they need a dumpster," Ten said.

We sat in silence, eating and drinking and thinking.

"Did he really have *six* cats?" I eventually asked Lisa. "I've only seen three so far. A big gray one, a Siamese, and a rather fluffy brown job."

She raised an eyebrow and of course I took the bait.

"I'm looking after them! In his greenhouse. The police put the beds outside, although I've no idea where everyone was sleeping. I've made a kind of 're-homing depot' and bought some cat-food."

"Good luck with that scheme," Lisa said. "Cats are out of fashion right now. Everyone seems to want small dogs."

"Little yappers," Ten muttered.

I grinned at him. "Don't be rude about them just because you're Great Dane size." I was thinking of poor homeless Hamburger. "Anyway, I've already found the Siamese one a new person. That policewoman wants him. Constable Moody."

"One down, five to go," Lisa said, nodding as though she was impressed. Then she spoiled it by adding, "So that's your spy headquarters?"

I shrugged and tried not to laugh. "Well it's *interesting*. I did find him, after all. I'd like to know more."

She gave an evil witchy cackle. "And you'll see everything they carry out of the house if you're skulking around in the garden."

"I won't be *skulking*," I protested. "Just visiting on a regular basis." I took another sip of my mango tea. Still very hot, but nicely fruity. "Someone has to look after them," I added.

"Are there any windows in the garage?" Ten asked. "If not, tell the cops to check it in case someone was after the cars." He blew on his drink.

I couldn't help thinking a car thief wouldn't turn up with a bow and arrow, but I suppose it would be quieter than a gun. "Even if there are windows, I bet they're covered up. All the house windows except the kitchen one have curtains pulled across so you can't see in."

Lisa sucked on her bottom lip. "What on earth was the old boy hiding?"

Silence fell as we all took another bite of our very nice muffins.

"I'm going to The Burkeville with Paul tonight," I finally said. "It'll be running hot with speculation. I hope no-one knows it was me who found Matthew."

Ten set down his mug. "Don't confirm or deny."

I shook my head, trying to remember details. "I'm still wondering why the front door wasn't locked. Did someone have a key? Did they do housework for him?" I slapped my forehead. "No, silly thought – from what I saw, you couldn't get in to do any."

"Was the lock broken?" Ten asked.

I looked across at him. "No idea. I didn't notice on the way in, and I certainly wasn't stopping to check on the way out. I probably smashed Olympic records when I ran for the doorway after finding him."

"You'll have to ask Bruce Carver," Lisa said. "Or the policewoman you've given the cat to."

"Yes, she might tell me," I agreed. (Always supposing she was still there.) I'd presumed there'd be a forensics team taking over and sifting through everything. Well, not through all the old newspapers, because they were plainly just old newspapers, but maybe once they'd thrown them into the dumpster and got the doors open to the rest of the rooms...

"I wonder if whoever wanted to burgle him got stymied by the barricades of paper? Simply couldn't get into wherever they planned to?" I thought about that for a few moments. "But they could have broken a window, of course."

Ten rubbed his big bristly chin. "Too noisy."

Lisa peeled herself away from his side. "Keep us informed," she said, leaning forward to gather up the plates and mugs as soon as we'd finished. She set them on the tray. I felt as though I was being dismissed, but if she'd worked all morning I could see she might want to spend some time with her newly re-acquired husband.

I stood. "I might do one more trip to Paradise Road."

"Summerfield of MI5," she teased.

"To check on the cats! If the first three have eaten all the food then any others who turn up will need more." Well, it sounded like a fair excuse to me.

She smirked at my protestation. "Three black ones."

"Really? Why are they all black?"

Lisa rolled her eyes. "It's a sad truth that in this age of social media most people don't want black cats because all you can see in photos are their eyes. Or no eyes at all if they've gone to sleep. Spotty cats and striped cats are much more photogenic."

Well that wasn't fair at all!

"I can't see social media being Matthew's thing," Ten said. "Not really mine, either. Just as well Mac's interested or the auto repair depot wouldn't have a website."

Lisa gave an enraged sniff. "Yes it would. I'd have made sure of it."

Ten sat up a foot taller. "It's not your business."

"It supports my family," she snapped.

I sighed inwardly. I couldn't leave them going at it hammer and tongs again. "Hey!" I said loudly. "Be nice to each other or I won't tell you all the dirty details once I discover them. And remember Pete can probably hear you."

I did my best to glare at them before I left the room. It was quite satisfying. Bossy little Lisa and big strong Ten Ton stared at me with half-open mouths. Yay me!

———

17 PARADISE ROAD was a hive of activity when I arrived. I heaved the jumbo-size pack of Fortune Kitty off the passenger seat and onto my hip, then made my way in past the gate which someone had chocked open with a couple of bricks. Of course I peered into the big yellow dumpster on my way in. It was already partly filled with newspapers and magazines that were being carried out in armloads by a team of people wearing white overalls. The old ink had made their arms smudgy. I really couldn't imagine there'd be any fantastic clues hidden between all those sheets of ageing paper but obviously they were doing a thorough search. They'd be at it for days at this rate!

To my surprise Bess Moody was still on duty, now holding a clipboard and noting who arrived and left.

"I got a cage," she said jubilantly. "I phoned the Animal Shelter and Lurline dropped it off here, so that was nice of her."

(Or she didn't want another cat to look after, I couldn't help thinking.)

I put the pack of Fortune Kitty on the ground and pulled the tab at the top open again. "You could store some of this in one of your pockets," I said. "In case you need to tempt Siam into the cage."

She took a handful of kibble and hid it away. "Good idea. I'm a novice at this."

Sensing she could do with all the encouragement I could provide, I added, "If he's anything like our dogs then he'll only need food and a warm bed." I peered along the strip of land between the house and the garage. "I've just been at Lisa Smedley's and she says there should be another three cats here somewhere – all black ones."

Bess Moody shook her head. "Haven't seen them. Mind you, I'm keeping clear of the greenhouse so I don't spook Siam."

Heaving the pack of food up again, I said, "I'll report back to you if he's there. I thought I'd better top up the dish in case it's all gone."

She gave me a mock-salute. "Carry on cat feeder! I can't wait to get my lovely moggy home. I hope he likes me." She flicked a few crumbs of Fortune Kitty off her fingers. "No – wouldn't want a black one. They never look good in Instagram photos."

So Lisa was right. Poor old pussies – judged by the color of their coats. It was a good thing Mathew had been too old for Instagram.

I trundled up the side of the house toward the greenhouse, glancing sideways at the garage as I went. Yes, long enough for two cars end-to-end if they weren't huge vehicles. Very obvious padlocks either side of the front door – a giveaway it was worth burgling, in my opinion. One small window, well off the ground, and the view inside blocked with what looked like a flattened cardboard carton which had once held cans of Wattie's peas. Goodness, that had to be old – I couldn't remember the last time I'd eaten canned peas. One door at the rear with another padlock.

I made a mental note to find Bruce Carver or Marian Wick and pass on Ten Ton Smedley's info about the cars. As the garage still looked locked, maybe they didn't know the contents were probably worth more than the house.

When I reached the greenhouse I found Feline HQ had gained a cat. Yes, a black one. Rather an old one too, to judge by its shaky gait and spindly legs. Skinnyblack, I decided, wondering if there'd be a Fatblack or if other names would suggest themselves when I located the final two.

Siam had laid claim to the furthest bed and was doing an athletic bottom-wash, one long leg in the air. He gave a hoarse yowl, but it seemed to be more a greeting than a complaint. Peanut was nowhere in sight. Fifty was curled up tightly in the center of the biggest bed. I wondered what sort of wars that would start once sharing was required. Old

Skinnyblack was sniffing the now-empty plant saucer and looking hard done by.

"Hang on, Puss," I said, putting the pack of food down on the grass and wishing I'd bought something to dole it out with. I lifted one of the small plastic flower pots off the shelf. Better than nothing. The cats were so keen that Siam stopped washing, mid-lick, Fifty immediately woke up, Skinnyblack planted his or her feet on the saucer and ended up with a tide of kibble around them, and Peanut came dashing out of the shrubbery. Poor things – they really were famished.

Duty done, I returned the Fortune Kitty to the car and headed for the front door of the house, hoping once again to waylay DS Bruce Carver or Marian Wick and pass on Ten Smedley's information. I was prevented from entering by WPC Moody. Yes, no more friendly 'Bess'. She can go back to her official title if she's going to be mean.

"Very active crime scene," she said. "Sorry, Merry – no entry by anyone unauthorized."

"But I found him."

"And I'm sure he still looks much the same."

I clutched my throat and grimaced. "What? He's still sitting at the kitchen table?"

She nodded grimly. "Yorkie Henderson and I – and those paramedics – really got a bollocking for moving the old girl in the church. Even though we were only doing it to spare her sister's feelings. Thank heavens Yorkie had taken photos." She gnawed on her bottom lip. "At least that was relatively straightforward. One victim, some bloodied carpet in a nice clean church, a broken vase, and a big bunch of flowers."

I had to agree. "And by comparison, this place is crammed. Yes, I suppose they can't risk missing anything. The kitchen would give a health inspector nightmares."

"Excuse us," an overall-clad person said as two of them tried to get past us with armloads of newspapers. We stepped aside.

Moody's eyes bulged. "Was it unhygienic?"

"It didn't *smell*," I said, trying to remember. "No – not smelly, but everything piled up everywhere. Stacks of pans and dishes. Heaps of packets. You could have a look through the window."

"Really?" Her eyes went wide.

"Oh – well – um – probably," I mumbled.

Darn – I hadn't meant to give away the fact I'd already had a little spy through it. I scratched my chin, attempting to look thoughtful. "There must *be* a window. The arrow was all lit up and shiny –"

She just about fell over at that revelation. "*Arrow?* I thought he was shot. The DS definitely said he was shot."

I cleared my throat. Goodness, they really were keeping things confidential. I dropped my volume way down. "Yes, but shot with an arrow. Okay, I've said that much now so I'll tell you the rest, but maybe you need to keep quiet about it until they release that info."

She nodded enthusiastically. The same two paper-carriers returned empty handed to collect their next load so I waited until they were inside the house again.

"He's sitting on a chair at the kitchen table. There's an arrow in his back." I swallowed, reliving the scene. "A long silver arrow. I assume it got him through the heart and he died instantly because he didn't look as though he'd tried to get up."

Although what would I know?

However, he'd still had the can of cat food and the opener on the table, and from my very quick glimpse before I panicked and rushed away, that seemed a reasonable assumption.

"Anyway," I said as something chimed in my brain, "You said 'one victim' in the church. Have they found someone else here besides Matthew?"

She shrugged. Looked down at her feet. "No, I don't think so. The brass have really got everything locked down tight. Euw, that's pretty weird. The arrow, I mean."

I nodded morosely. Had I ever heard of anyone being dispatched that way? Not since Graham had read me Robin Hood stories out loud when I was a scaredy-cat five and he was a bloodthirsty twelve year old. I've no idea how he graduated from that to being a fussy stamp-collecting lawyer.

There was still no sign of the detectives. "More than one way to skin a cat," I said, although that was possibly an unfortunate choice of phrase given the current situation. "Listen along if you like," I said to Moody, wrestling my phone out of my jeans pocket and letting her see I was scrolling to Bruce Carver's number. Her eyes went wide and she covered her mouth with her hand.

"Carver!" He didn't sound at all relaxed. "What is it, Ms Summerfield?"

"Sorry to bother you, Detective, but I promised Ten Ton Smedley I'd pass this on to you. Ten who owns Drizzle Bay Auto Repairs?"

"Yes-yes." Boy, stress central!

I stood up straighter. "Matthew Boatman had two very valuable old classic cars. Worth a real heap. Do you know if they're still here in the garage, because we wondered if they might be the motivation for his murder. The garage still looks locked, though."

There was a moment of seething silence. Maybe I heard his teeth grinding?

"Thank you Ms Summerfield." Didn't sound like he'd unclenched his jaw yet.

I tried again. "I mean hundreds of thousands of dollars. Two very old, very special Alfa Romeos."

A long infuriated sigh. "We'll look into it, never fear."

"Have you found his keys? I'm sure they weren't in the front door."

"THANK you, Ms Summerfield," he grated. "In this mess we'd be lucky to find our own faces." He disconnected without another word.

Bess Moody and I raised our eyebrows at each other.

I glanced at my watch. "I'd better go home and do some work. I promised myself I'd finish editing a children's book by tonight so I could have Sunday free. Have you got any nieces or nephews who like Elaine O'Blythe's stories?"

"The animal ones?" she asked, whacking her thigh with the clipboard as though she needed to warm herself up.

I wasn't surprised if her legs were going to sleep, having to wait around like this on a cold concrete step. "Yes. She does all the pretty paintings too."

Moody changed hands and whacked the other leg a few times.

I dropped my volume as though I was sharing top-secret news. "Elaine will have another one out soon. I'd better not tell you more than that because authors can get a bit precious about titles and covers and so on until launch day."

She nodded as though that made sense. Then her mouth fell open and her eyes widened. "The Orphan Cats of Paradise Road!" she exclaimed. "Lots of animals. Wouldn't that make a great title? Siam could model for her."

"The Orphan Cats of Paradise Road," I repeated, nodding slowly. "It has a definite ring to it. I could even suggest it to her."

"Please?" she asked. "I think it sounds fantastic."

I grinned at her enthusiasm, jingled the car keys, and waved goodbye. I'll bet you anything she crept around the corner of the house and peered in through the kitchen window the moment she thought it was safe to.

7

BIRDS AND PEES

THE SPANIELS WERE ecstatic to have some company and I spent five minutes throwing their two balls the length of the back lawn. Two dogs, two balls, two separate sprints and retrievals, no arguments. Very slobbery hands, though, by the time I'd had enough of the game.

After a good wash, and with Graham still not home from golf, I made myself a cheese and chutney sandwich on whole-wheat bread and opened my laptop to do a little research. One early muffin from Iona's and one late one at Lisa's didn't feel like quite enough for lunch, and I didn't want my tum gurgling in an unladylike manner while I was in the car with Paul on the way to The Burkeville. I munched happily as I started to research the toilet habits of birds.

Yes, truly! My lovely dyslexic author – Elaine O'Blythe – writes brilliant children's books. Her grammar and spelling are both atrocious, but because her storytelling is amazing I always enjoy putting my editing efforts into reshaping her work. I felt sure this would be another winner for her.

She'd titled it "Birds Can't Pee". How could any child resist a title like that?

I wondered if birds could or couldn't pee. I should have asked Lisa; she'd know about chickens and turkeys anyway. Hopefully Mr Google would know about other bird species.

Elaine had described how Taimana and Maaka, two little fantailed *Piwakawaka*, had noticed cows and horses peeing onto the grass of the farm fields. (Don't you immediately picture a small boy's eyes lighting up?)

All Taimana and Maaka could do was poop. They sat together discussing the situation and wondering if it was a problem.

Elaine had woven it into a gorgeous tale – with lots of farm information and general countryside lore along with her trademark whimsical watercolor paintings.

And now she had me wondering! Had I ever seen a bird pee? Ummmm...?

Mr Google explained how birds cleverly combined the two functions in one orifice. Birds don't pee, they soft-poop. A lot. Landing on a branch or the top of a fence often jolts it out.

OMG – I really hadn't needed to know that, but Elaine was definitely correct.

I was munching the last of my sandwich and snorting with giggles – as silly as any six year old – when I heard a flurry of barking and the garage door rolling up. My brother

Graham's big Mercedes is whisper-quiet, but the garage door has a definite squeak. I swallowed my last bite, wondering if he'd won his ten dollars back from Maurie Jacobs. From the time he took to come inside, and the boisterous barks from the yard, I suspect Manny and Dan were treated to another big session of fetch-the-ball.

"All good?" I asked when he poked his head around the doorframe of my office. Lawyer Graham isn't much given to having fun. He gets great pleasure from his dogs, and a round of golf, and possibly from Susan Hammond, the on and-off friend he keeps very quiet about. He's a serious man but willing to impart information if you ask him the right way. I wanted some info on Matthew Boatman.

"All very good indeed," he confirmed, hitching the waist of his plaid golfing slacks higher. "I won my money back, had an enjoyable game, an excellent lunch, and I think I'll put my feet up and watch the rugby now. You working? I'll keep the volume down."

I pushed my chair back from the desk. "Just Googling a bit of info." I certainly wouldn't be telling Graham the topic! "I do – um – have some bad news I'm afraid. Was Matthew Boatman a client of yours?"

He put on his thinking face, eyes directed toward the ceiling and finger tapping his chin. "Boatman... Boatman... unusual name." His finger left his chin and he raised it triumphantly. "Old cars. Went to Africa."

That was a surprise. "Did he? When? To live there? I've seen him around Drizzle Bay for years."

Graham nodded, and reached down to pat Manny who was nudging at his knee. "Yonks ago now. I seem to remember his wife didn't like it there so they came back after a while. I think I put some preparatory work into a divorce settlement for them but I don't recall it going ahead."

I closed my laptop, rather surprised by that. "She died a long time ago. That's probably why."

He nodded, looking distracted, eyeing the plate I'd had my sandwich on. "Something snacky would do me for dinner, Merry. We had a big lunch."

Oh good – that let me off cooking duty. "You can make yourself a sandwich when you're ready, then. There's plenty of bread and cheese and cold meat and pickles." I practically saw him filing away a mental list as though there was a recipe. "Paul McCreagh's taking me to The Burkeville. And if we can get back to Matthew Boatman for a minute... I said I had some bad news. He's dead. I found him when I was collecting for the Red Cross this morning."

Graham was across the room in an instant with his arm around my shoulders. "Sis – no – how awful for you!"

Sis is his biggest term of endearment so I tilted my head and rested it against the solid cage of his ribs for a few seconds. At least he didn't say, 'not another one'.

I drew a deep breath of ironed shirt, woolen jersey, and Old Spice. "Sitting at his kitchen table. Shot. The Police have said that much but I guess there'll be more news to follow." I sat up straighter again. "Actually, what will it matter if I tell you? You're the most discreet person I know. He was shot in the back with an arrow."

"Good grief!" Graham exclaimed, pushing Manny away from his knee and giving me his whole attention. "Oh Sis. Nasty. Really nasty. Are you coping okay?"

I shrugged at that. "Well, what's the option? Falling to pieces? Not really my style, is it? I'll be fine, Jeepie. I got past the others." I rolled my office chair back and rose to my feet.

He cracked a smile at my pet name for him. I don't use it often. Jeepie for GP — Graham Patrick Summerfield. "Good that you'll have some company this evening, then," he agreed.

"Except they'll probably all badger me with questions if they find out it was me." I pulled my ponytail band off and shook my hair loose. "Again."

Graham picked up my plate to take to the kitchen. Did I also say he's a fanatical tidy-upper? "I meant the vicar," he said, winking and turning away.

Hmm. I hadn't expected that. My brother is such an unromantic man with his on-again off-again Susan connection. Maybe there was more to that than I suspected? Perhaps he was the last of the red hot lovers disguised in his perpetual charcoal suit and white shirt and royal blue 'trust me' tie?

But then I pictured his sturdy freckled hands with the tufts of pale hair on the backs of his fingers as he sorted through his precious stamps. It took only a few seconds' comparison with Paul McCreagh's and John Bonnington's long, tanned fingers and I dismissed that idea. Dependable – yes. Desirable – no. Sorry bro.

Although who was I to decide that? I'd made the bad mistake of marrying Duncan Skeene, who now seemed to have nothing at all to recommend him. What had I seen in him all those years ago?

———

KNOWING I probably couldn't settle into serious editing with Matthew's murder on my mind I went and changed my boots for the old sneakers I preferred to walk in. There was no way I was wrecking my quite new suede boots in the sand. I put my head around the doorframe of the room where Graham was watching the rugby. "I'm going for an amble on the beach to try and unwind. Want to come with me?"

He tore his gaze away from the big TV screen long enough to say, "No thanks, Sis. I walked all morning at golf. Already gone miles."

Manny and Dan had both raised their muzzles at the mention of a walk, but as it was only me who was saying 'walk' they immediately lost interest again. Having their master's attention for the rest of the afternoon beat anything I could offer.

I glanced out of the window; it was still fine, but a frisky breeze whipped the vegetation to and fro and had spume trailing from the tops of the waves. My old jersey was warm – a past birthday present hand-knitted by our lovely departed mother, Sally, but it was no match for that wind. "Okay, I'll just grab a jacket. Won't be too long."

"Take as long as you need," Graham said, turning his attention back to the rugby as one of the Barrett boys dived over the line between the goalposts. "You beauty!" he yelled, and the dogs howled their glee as well.

Leaving them to it, I headed to the hall cupboard where the outdoor coats lived. I pulled on my quilted red puffer jacket, slid my keys into one of its pockets, zipped them safely inside, and let myself out of the house.

Then I stood for a few moments, breathing the salty air deep into my lungs and trying to regain my usual not-too-worried-about-anything mood. Honestly, I really do believe people have the power to talk themselves in and out of things more than they realize.

It was time I talked myself out of my mournful thoughts. I'd grown up here. Knew many of the people, most of the houses, lots of the dogs. Peaceful, drowsy, Drizzle Bay; yet it was now the scene of three murders.

I couldn't remember anything so savage happening in the past. Sure, the odd drunken fight on Saturday nights, traffic accidents sometimes as drivers underestimated the speed of others as they tried to merge on the main highway, but basically no-one died here except of natural causes.

Now there were three murders and I'd been involved with every one of them.

I tried to squash the sick sensation in my throat, rubbed my fizzy tummy for a few seconds, shook my head, and walked briskly across the road. Surely if I told myself often enough and firmly enough that it was total co-incidence then I'd start to believe it?

Wouldn't I?

The sea tossed and roared, driving onto the beach in long white-capped rollers, and I expected to see surfers in wetsuits making the most of it. How they don't feel the cold, I can't imagine. Sure enough, three of them were visible – two flat on their boards and another looking as though he should have been up at the surf championships at Raglan. Flashy for sure, but I couldn't help admiring the confident twists and turns as he wove to and fro, balanced to perfection. Then, as he neared the sand, he turned as he stepped off the board and I saw his long fall of dirty-blond hair. John Bonnington – all height and muscle and Californian drawl. He was at least a hundred yards away, but he raised an arm in greeting so I did the same. Maybe he had 40/40 vision? Is that even a thing? Do Black Ops assassins need especially good eyesight? (Not that I have definitive proof that John is an assassin. I'm much more suspicious about Erik.)

I glanced at my watch. Erik would need him back at The Burkeville for the Saturday night rush pretty soon. As I thought about that, John strode up the sand, board under his arm, and disappeared along the path through the scruffy *ngaio* trees and tussocks. No doubt his black pick-up truck was in the parking bay close by. And also no doubt I'd see him later tonight, charming the local ladies as he tended the bar in a muscle-revealing T-shirt, all that blond hair wound up in a man-bun, and his amazing blue eyes dancing and watchful by turns. John Bonnington is a total babe magnet. I should put him out of my mind.

The trouble is he gave me the best kiss of my life. Yes, I *know* he was taking pity on me because my ex, Duncan, arrived at The Burkeville with a much younger woman and turned on a pretty sickening display of affection toward her in front of me. John had swooped in, pretending to be delighted to see me, all tanned muscles and Jon Bon Jovi hair, purred my name in that lazy accent. And planted a fake 'welcome home' kiss on my lips that we both enjoyed very much.

It lasted far too long.

Duncan definitely noticed.

I'd had John down as being Detective Marian Wick's lover (I do have an inventive brain) so I was really surprised he could turn on such apparently ardent attention for anyone else. But after one toe-curling kiss and a cheery wave, he departed, leaving me thrilled and throbbing and thoroughly confused. I've been reliving it for months.

I gave my head a sharp shake. Plainly I'm still reliving it. I need to get him out of my system.

8

A RAMBLE WITH LORD DRIZZLE

"Little Merry!" That cheery, gravelly voice from under the battered hat had to be Lord Jim Drizzle, and sure enough, when I stepped down past a big sheltering *toi toi* plant, there he was – stumping along in the sand, and accompanied by his old black and white collie, Lizzie.

"Uncle Jim!" He's not my uncle, but he was a good friend of our Dad, and ever since I was five or six I've called him that.

A stronger than usual gust of wind roared by, causing the *toi toi's* long thin leaves to lash around like a many-tailed whistling whip. Old Lizzie glared at it and gave it a warning growl.

"Easy girl, easy girl," his Lordship murmured, leaning down to give her a couple of hefty pats on her hairy back.

"You're a long way from home," I suggested. Drizzle Farm is a couple of miles away – at the junction of Drizzle Bay

Road and Drizzle Beach Road (and who made up those stupid names? No wonder I got totally lost when I went to pet-sit Isobel Crombie's little dogs out that way).

He fixed his affectionate gaze on me. "Zinnia broke a tooth. I drove her in to get it fixed."

"On a Saturday afternoon?"

Jim tapped the side of his nose. "Eddie Parsons is her sister's son. He knows to give his aunt preferential treatment or his mother would be very displeased."

"Poor Lady Zin," I said. "Dentists' visits are not my favorite thing."

Jim nodded morosely. "Or hers. But she said it had a very sharp point that kept catching on her tongue."

"Oh, nasty." I fell into step beside him, wondering how best to approach the subject of my third body. We ambled on in silence until I simply blurted, "Did you know Matthew Boatman?"

Matthew and Lord Jim would have been much of an age. I'd be surprised if they weren't acquainted. But had His Lordship heard about the murder yet?

Apparently not. "Eye-tie Boatman?" he asked, waggling his fierce hairy eyebrows at me.

I stared at him, probably squinting in the rushing salty air. The nickname was hardly PC these days! "Why do you call him that?"

"He used to race Italian cars. Utterly fixated on them."

That was unexpected. I was used to seeing old Matthew in his gardening hat, snipping shrubbery into shape, and now I had to adjust to a new picture of him – in one of those old-fashioned racing helmets, tearing around the kind of ill-designed tracks that had claimed so many lives in the past.

"Goodness," I said, while I dredged up something more appropriate. "And this was at the same places you raced?"

Did I tell you I'm editing Lord Drizzle's memoirs? This was intended to be 'something for the family', but once he got the bit between his teeth there's been no stopping him. Some farm history of course, the strange story about how he became a lord because there were no family members left in England to inherit the title, and his first time voting in the British House of Lords. That's all I'd expected really.

But heavens to Betsy, off he went about his early days as a motor cycle racer, with all sorts of famous names included. Giacomo Agostini of Italy who won fifteen Motorcycle World Championships in the mid-sixties and seventies. Cecil Sandford of the United Kingdom who won two between 1952 and 1957, when Jim would surely have been a teenager.

Cecil Sandford! Cecil! Did you ever hear a less likely name for someone kitted out in black leather, screaming around on a stinky death-machine?

Barely stopping to draw breath Jim had then sprinted sideways and given his opinion of The Rabbit Destruction Council, after their mesh fences to halt the tide of bunnies taking over the best kiwi farmland had failed. Then he switched to pig-hunting in the hills behind Drizzle Bay before the huge pine plantations were laid out.

Onward to Lady Zinnia's painting abilities, descriptions of her entries for several years of the Kelliher Art Prize (sadly she was never the winner) and then his granddaughter's creation for the World of Wearable Arts last year – a Japanese kimono-like garment made entirely of sheet-metal and rivets. Back to some scathing thoughts on deer-farming for velvet, considered an aphrodisiac in some countries, but a theory he poured cold water on. (Had he tried it? I boggled a bit at that thought.) A quick U-turn to describe the benefits of once-a-day milking, a long discussion on the merits of different breeds of sheep, then off to the House of Lords again and the enormous scaffolding job he'd seen around Big Ben.

He was all over the place, but both chatty and interesting. I'm having a heck of a time trying to arrange the assorted topics into any coherent order, let alone taming his florid writing style.

"Yes, same racetracks," he said, breaking into my rambling thoughts. Honestly, I'm as bad as he is.

"But you raced bikes and he raced cars?" I asked, recovering my train of thought.

He bent and picked up a hefty stick, hurling it out across the sand for old Lizzie. She trundled after it at a sedate pace and carried it in her jaws for a few minutes before losing interest and dropping it.

Jim turned back to me. "I never raced cars," he confirmed. "Always liked the wind in my face."

I thought of the Italian-sounding cars Ten Ton Smedley

had mentioned. "Not what I expected of Matthew." Then I asked with trepidation, "Have you had the radio on today?"

Jim shook his head. "Rotary-hoed some of the kitchen garden for Zinnia and planted a couple of rows of late potatoes. Did a bit of welding. Gave Denny and Joe a hand to crutch some of the ewes before they drop their lambs. All a bit noisy for the radio."

I swallowed. "Ah," I said, "So you won't know that Matthew was found dead today. Shot in his kitchen."

Jim stopped walking and stared at me. Clamped a big rough hand on his chest. I hoped he wasn't on the verge of a heart attack, but he turned the tables by clearing his throat and declaring, "Not surprised. He's been asking for it for years."

"*What?*" I more or less shrieked.

(*'Don't say 'what' darling,' my dead mother reminded me.*)

Lord Jim lowered his bristling brows and muttered a few things between clamped teeth that I had no hope of hearing. Then he said with more volume; "He had no idea how to treat a woman. He dragged his poor wife off to Africa – Zimbabwe I think – totally against her will, and pregnant. She was lucky to survive the birth of their son. Never had any others."

Huh??? Inoffensive old Matthew? No idea how to treat a woman? He tipped his hat at me every time he saw me. And surely I hadn't been singled out for the only hat-tipping in Drizzle Bay? "What did he go to Africa for?"

"Prospecting for minerals, or so the story went." Jim

twitched his plaid scarf more snugly around his neck.

"So he was a geologist?" I hadn't a clue – I'd never known him as anything except an old chap who toddled around the garden and village, nodding benignly.

Jim let out a long, slow considering noise. "More precious stones than iron ore and coal – or whatever geologists search for these days."

"They're after rare earths. Which are also precious."

Jim peered at me from under the brim of his hat. "What do they grow in those?"

Well darn – I wasn't going to be able to describe that very well. "Nothing at all. They make parts for computers and so on out of them. I read somewhere recently that's why they want to get to Mars."

He made a noise that sounded very like "Pshaw!"

"The scientists think there are more rare earths there. Elements with strange names, Uncle Jim. Way beyond me to know about or be able to explain to you."

"Rare earths," he scoffed. "No – I meant things like diamonds and sapphires and so on."

The back of my neck prickled. My hair was pulled firmly into a ponytail but I'm sure all the little hairs there would have risen up and waved in the wind otherwise.

Diamonds and sapphires?

Matthew had been a gem hunter. And his daughter-in-law, Jude Boatman, and her fancy gold-printed business cards, was a gemologist! Heavens to Betsy, this put a different complexion on things.

I tried to contain my excitement and asked in my best bored voice, "Do you think he found any?"

Jim cleared his throat. "Well those Italian cars of his didn't come cheap."

Indeed. Even though they were pretty old now, Ten Ton Smedley had put outrageous price estimates on them. Always supposing they were the same vehicles, of course. He might have driven something much cheaper, earlier on.

"And his wife died?" I asked, thinking of Graham's comments about a possible divorce that hadn't been followed through with.

"Years ago now. Nice woman. Shy little thing."

I reached down and gave Lizzie a pat while I considered that. Lizzie immediately subjected my hands to a big sniffing session. Plainly The Orphan Cats of Paradise Road were still hanging around on my skin, despite a good hand-wash after throwing the balls for the dogs and before making my sandwich. Or maybe she could smell traces of Manny and Dan? I wondered what Lizzie would make of the myriad elderly smells at Matthew's old house. I also wondered how the Police were getting on with their clean-out. Had they broken through the wall of newspapers yet?

"Did you know he was a hoarder?" I asked, squinting up at Jim. The sun was low now the afternoon was getting late.

Jim shook his head. "Doesn't seem likely from his tidy front yard."

"No – but inside the house. There's stuff piled everywhere. The main hallway was totally blocked by stacks of newspapers that go back forever. They're clearing it out so they can get the doors open and see what's in the rest of the place."

Jim looked at me as though I was telling fibs.

"Truly! He has all the curtains pulled across so you can't see in from the outside." A sudden thought struck me. "Do you think he has a hidden stash of diamonds in there?"

Lizzie gave a low growl and thrust her wet nose up my sleeve.

"Out of there, Lizzie," Jim ordered, pushing the old dog away. "I'm sure they'll find them if he has. It strikes me as unlikely, though."

I wiped my hand on the leg of my jeans. "I wonder what Lizzie can smell? Probably a cat. Matthew had no less than six of them, and I'm in charge of finding new homes for them if I can."

"A cat-hoarder, too," Jim suggested, and we both started laughing as we resumed our walk along the sand.

"Well, I've re-located one of them, anyway," I called over the wind. "To a policewoman who's working there. Only five more to go."

We strode on for another fifteen minutes – at which time Jim checked his watch and declared he'd better get back 'toot sweet' to collect Lady Zin from the dentist.

"Are you late?" I asked.

He scrunched up his face. "Possibly. But I'm sure she can fill in a few minutes at that new shop Belinda Butterfly has next to her bridal place."

Yes, I'll bet she could. Belinda has told me privately she does well there from Saturday customers.

"Shall we walk back along the road?" I suggested. "It might be faster than plowing through this sand?"

We fought our way up the slope and through the tussocks until we reached the smooth asphalt surface.

"A hoarder?" Jim muttered, yanking his hat on more firmly. "I really didn't picture the old boy with stacks of stuff inside that house."

"Or dead?" I suggested. "Still sitting at his kitchen table. I'm sure the TV News will be all over it tonight. And the Coastal Courier, too. Bob Burgess was grilling the police-woman who's adopted the cat there as soon as the murder became common knowledge."

"Good little paper, that," Jim said. "Definitely has its finger on the pulse of the village."

I held my tongue. I'd provided quite a few local snippets to Bob on the condition my name wasn't associated with them. Who'd talk to me then? A sudden thought hit: could I get some free publicity for the cats that needed homes? Right now Matthew was hot news, so to speak.

As soon as I'd waved goodbye to Jim and Lizzie I dug out my phone and started composing a persuasive text. I sent it off to Bob and headed home to get my car. Those cats would be getting an early meal so I could make myself look presentable for dinner at The Burkeville with a certain yummy vicar. Not to mention I'd like to check how fast those newspapers were disappearing from Matthew's hallway...

9

DINNER FOR EVERYONE

DIAMONDS AND SAPPHIRES? Well, that made a decent motive –
if Matthew had any stashed away. As his daughter-in-law was
a gemologist I could see why she was keen to gain entry and
get her hands on them. Although she was probably the bene-
ficiary of his will if his wife was dead, his sister was dead, and
his son was dead. That was a lot of dead people. His sister
and his wife might have been elderly, but his son? I needed
to check with Graham and see what he knew. Of course old
Matthew might have left the lot for the care of his cats...

I was out of luck with the newspapers though. I saw the
big yellow dumpster was almost half full of them when I
peered in, but there was a uniformed security guard who
levered himself out of a nearby pickup truck the moment I
tried to get in the gate.

"Hold it right there, Madam!" (Not even 'Miss'. I must be
showing my age.)

"I've come to feed all the cats," I said, heaving the bag of Fortune Kitty higher on my hip.

He pulled his head back, which meant his rather thick neck transformed into several chins. I wondered if he was a weightlifter with his chunky build. Either he was solid muscle from lots of fitness routines or solid fat from too much sitting in vehicles and eating pies and donuts from paper bags. Maybe the fat theory won, because he was a real waddler once he got going.

"The deceased had six cats," I elaborated. "Detective Bruce Carver has asked me to keep them fed and to find new homes for them. They're around the back of the house."

I must have summoned up enough authority to impress him because he actually opened the gate for me. Then I saw why; it was padlocked, although anyone a bit fitter than me could easily have vaulted over. Both the fence and gate were fashioned from curly black wrought iron and provided a good view through to the neatly clipped bushes Matthew had been so proud of.

The guard insisted on accompanying me up the side path as far as Feline HQ. Maybe he was pleased to have something to do besides sitting in the car? I'm sure I didn't look like a threat, clutching my bag of kibble.

Where the path narrowed he moved in front of me and peered sideways as though there might be danger lurking around the back of the old house.

"So have they all gone for the day?" I asked.

"Meal break," he said. "They'll be back."

I glanced at my watch. It was just after five. "All of them went together?"

He shrugged his huge shoulders. "Guess it gets it over and done with in one go."

I tend to forget how regimented some organizations are. As a freelance editor I'm absolutely my own boss and can arrange my life as I wish. This might sometimes mean relaxed lunches at Iona's Café, but those days are balanced against late evenings pounding away at my keyboard and getting eyestrain from peering at the screen when the work comes in thick and fast.

We rounded the corner and the greenhouse came into view. A sudden brilliant thought flashed into my mind. "Would you like a cat?" I asked, peering at his badge. It said Vinny Waitomo.

"A free one?"

"Yes, of course, Vinny. Let's see who's here." I held up a hand for caution and then waved at the sleeping quarters. We crept forward, checking out the occupants through the somewhat dusty panes of glass. Siam was gone of course, but big solid Fifty was curled into a ball and sound asleep. Skinnyblack looked up and glared at us, and Peanut rolled over in the biggest bed and did an athletic and graceful stretch.

"My little girl would love that striped one," Vinny Waitomo said. "She's been asking for a kitten, but we live on a busy road."

"Wrong time of the year for kittens," I said, thinking of

Bess Moody's pronouncement. "They mostly get born in the summer."

Vinny rubbed his waterfall of chins. "I wouldn't risk a kitten with the traffic past home, anyway. A full-grown cat would be a better idea."

I nodded at his wisdom. "What's your daughter's name?"

A smile stretched his lips, and two rows of dazzling white teeth almost blinded me. Fond dad, for sure. "Poppy. And she's as pretty as one."

I couldn't help laughing. "Poppy and Peanut. Perfect. Although she could choose her own name," I added quickly. "The cat wouldn't know."

Someone must have heard the kibble moving in the bag because suddenly everyone was awake and alert. Peanut sat up and did some tail-swishing. Skinnyblack gave a plaintive meow. Fifty unrolled and added to the chorus. Another black cat bolted out from the shrubbery and joined in. It was hard to be sure but I think it only had one eye. Big voice though!

"You've got your work cut out," Vinny Waitomo said, pushing the greenhouse door aside for me. Even the awful screeching it made didn't scare the cats away.

I waded in through a sea of furry bumping heads, every cat encouraging me to tip the Fortune Kitty out faster. Their enthusiasm was rewarded by a shower of kibble on their ears.

"Poor things are very hungry," Vinny Waitomo said, peering closer.

"They just don't want the others getting more than

them," I said. "I fed them around lunchtime once Mr Boatman's body was discovered. I think they'd been without food for a whole day though."

His face assumed a very mournful expression, mouth turned down and brow wrinkled. Plainly a day without food was a terrible prospect for Vinny. And now I'd spent a little longer in his company I was pretty sure about the 'too much eating in cars' scenario over the 'muscles from the gym' theory.

As soon as everyone's head was down in the big saucer and the greenhouse was full of crunching noises, I said to him, "Are you serious about a cat for Poppy? If you are, I'll reserve one for you."

"The striped one."

"Yes. Peanut. Or whatever your Poppy wants to call her. I think it's a 'her'. She's quite small, and so pretty with all those stripes and ruffles."

Vinny pursed his lips. "Hopefully not a 'her' any longer."

"Indeed," I said in a dry tone, not wanting to get into a de-sexing cats conversation with a man I'd only just met.

He sent me the smile of a very fond Dad. "It's Poppy's sixth birthday on Wednesday. Can you keep the cat here that long?"

I nodded vigorously. "I'll make a list and pin it inside the glass so people know who's still available." This was going better than I'd expected. Two cats re-homed. Although, to be fair, I now had a very solid grey one left and three who were black – if the mysterious third black one ever showed up. They might not be so easy. Especially the single-eyed puss.

"Oh well," I said, folding over the top of the Fortune Kitty bag, "That's them done for now. I'll be back in the morning."

Vinny stepped aside so I could exit the little space, and I watched as he pulled the screeching door closed against the brick stopper. "Won't see you in the morning," he said. "I'm on nights."

What an awful prospect – stuck here at Paradise Road through all the dark hours ahead.

"What about your dinner?" I asked.

He slapped his tummy. "No worries. As soon as this crew comes back I'm off for a while. I don't take over again until they're ready to go for the night."

I nodded and turned away. And as I did I noticed the padlock on the door at the back of the garage was hanging loose. Someone had unlocked it and not pushed it home again. A prickle of anticipation ran up my spine.

I itched to take a look inside, and sauntered a few steps in that direction in case I could beat Vinny to the door. "Old Mr Boatman used to be a racing car driver. Did you know that?" I prattled over my shoulder. "Italian cars. He might still have one in here." I quickly slipped the padlock off and turned the doorknob.

"Hey," Vinny said. "That's not really on."

"It's unlocked," I said, eyes full of innocence. "Someone's working here so I'm not exactly breaking in. Ten Ton Smedley said it was a really expensive model – if it's still here of course." I pulled the door open with creak of hinges. "I've seen Mr Boatman around the village in a very shiny old car, but it didn't look like anything you'd race."

Vinny shook his head, but after a furtive glance around the yard he didn't try and stop me.

Inside the garage it was as black as a coalmine. The cardboard-covered window let in only the dimmest of glows, the front doors were still locked of course, and burly Vinny prevented much light entering from the back. A gleaming shape crouched in front of us, and even I recognized the Alfa Romeo crest – a dark blue circle with a snake on one half and a red cross on a white background on the other.

"See," I said to Vinny. "It says Alfa Romeo on top and Milano down the bottom." I reached toward it.

"Fingerprints!" Vinny snapped, and I whipped my hand back.

"You don't want anyone knowing you've been in here," he added. "And I don't want to have to tell them. You should give that padlock and door handle a wipe with your hankie, just in case."

He was certainly security-conscious. Ideal for the job, provided he didn't need to actually chase anyone. Although how was I to know he didn't have a hidden pistol or stun-gun about his large person?

I shook my head. Who was I kidding? Only myself. This is very-small-town New Zealand, where pea weevil infestations beat political scandals hands down, and if anyone has a gun it's mostly for shooting unfortunate wildlife.

"Mmm, thanks," I said, backing out of the garage. I set down the pack of Fortune Kitty and attempted to rub over the padlock with my jersey sleeve.

Vinny rolled his eyes and produced a large white handkerchief with blue striped borders, indicating he'd take over.

I picked up the Fortune Kitty again. "Thanks for thinking of it."

"Never worth letting anyone know you've been sniffing around where you shouldn't have been," he said, rubbing away as though he was intent on bringing the brass to a high shine.

"I'll probably see you tomorrow evening," I said by way of goodbye. "You could maybe ask if Lurline at the Animal Shelter has a cat cage you could borrow for transport?"

I gave him an airy wave, hoping I'd get a better look into the garage at feline breakfast time. Always supposing the padlock was still unlatched.

To my annoyance I found I had to wait inside the gate until dutiful Vinny appeared again and unlocked it for me. But never mind – the evening stretched before me with the promise of Paul's excellent company and a meal I wouldn't have to cook for myself. It was bound to be better than finding an old dead man and doling out dinner for a lot of hungry cats. Wasn't it?

10

HOT TUB AND TITTLE-TATTLE

GRAHAM and the spaniels were still watching TV when I returned.

Feeling I deserved a treat after my disconcerting day I pointed to the bathroom and he nodded. Then I ran an extravagantly deep bubble bath, looped my hair up over the back of the tub, and settled down to soak. If only it was as easy to wash away the memory of Matthew sitting in that chair as it was to sponge away the sea-spray from my skin...

I decided to do some serious thinking as I lay under the bubbles. Who wanted to kill Matthew? Why? What did he have bailed up behind all those newspapers? What was he doing with such an expensive car? Where did abrasive Jude Boatman fit into the story? What had happened to her husband – Matthew's only son? Who would want a one-eyed cat?

I suspect I drifted off for a while because I came to with a huge lurch and slopped water up the sides of the tub and over the bathroom floor. No useful answers had occurred to me. Yes, sound asleep, obviously. And now the ends of my hair were wet because I'd relaxed so far into the water some of it had joined me.

Cursing quietly, I heaved myself out of my soapy heaven.

Half an hour later I was clean, dry, and rattling hangers along my wardrobe rail in search of something slimming, glamorous, and comfortable. Nothing comfortable was slimming. Nothing glamorous felt comfortable. And, sadly, nothing looked slimming at all. Curse your delicious goodies, Iona, and your expectations of large and regular dinners, Graham!

I settled on my ever-handy burgundy skirt and a soft dove-grey jersey with a low scooped neckline. And a dangly necklace to draw some further attention to my two best features. I drew a brush through my hair until I'd unsnagged all the knots. Paul likes me to wear it down, but it had been windy on the beach so the trip from the front door to his car would probably turn it into a mess again. I gathered up the front half, secured it behind my head with a bronzy clip I'm fond of, and let the rest cascade down the back. If I couldn't see it, I wasn't too worried. Paul could always untangle the knots if he felt so inclined.

I should be so lucky.

Then I went to work on my make-up. Seriously went to work. Not only was I keen to move things on with one of the men in my life, but the memory of poor old Matthew sitting in his kitchen chair was spooking me out more and more as the time ticked by.

I really didn't want to look like a deflated and worried old hag. Carefree and good company was what I had in mind, so heaps of moisturizer to plump my skin up after the drying windy walk, a light but careful coating of foundation, and enough blusher to make me look more cheerful (although not so much my cheeks lit up like neon signs once I'd had a couple of drinks.)

Then the smoky eye. I wonder why they always describe it as singular in those on-line tutorials? The editor in me itches to make it plural. I fiddled around quite happily for a while, trying to strike the balance between two coal-holes in the snow and something shadowy and mysterious with long eyelashes. Maybe I won and maybe I didn't. I grabbed my coat and clutch.

Vicar Paul knocked on the door almost to the second, and I opened it to find darkness had fallen. What a dependable man he is! Would he drive me mad with his outwardly conservative ways, or might he surprise me totally if he felt he'd finally recovered from his PTSD and we took things a step or two further? Something to think on while we drove as far as The Burkeville Bar and Café.

I didn't get the chance. He'd no sooner closed the passenger-side door on me, solicitous Englishman that he is, than he was full of further questions about Matthew's death. Was I feeling okay? Had I got the shakes under control now? Had

I heard anything else while I was giving the cats their dinner?

Yes to the first two, and no to the third. "The cops had gone for a meal somewhere so there was no-one there apart from a security guard. I expect they'll all be back at the house by now, though. And I re-homed another cat."

I looked across at him. The headlamps of cars rushing by in the opposite direction lit up his wavy dark hair and silhouetted his perfectly straight nose. You'd think with all the games of basketball in Afghanistan, and now with his troop of trouble-maker schoolboys, someone might have banged it with an elbow and spoiled it, but no.

"I got a look at his Alfa Romeo," I added. "Ten says it's worth a fortune."

Paul's teeth gleamed as a car rushed by. "Be nice if he'd left Saint Agatha's some money. My fund for rebuilding the church hall is making very slow progress."

Yes, I knew it was. Several years ago the old tinder-dry wooden hall had been torched – possibly by the miscreant older brothers of the current basketball team. Since then the choice of anywhere to hold public meetings has been the church itself (not ideal), and Iona's café (also not ideal because it's a place of business, after all), or the school hall along in in Burkeville (rather too far away, and not quite on home ground). There'd been talk of using the disused shop next to Winston Bamber's upmarket gallery, but there are definitely mice there, and no proper tea- making facilities or chairs. No-one has dredged up quite enough enthusiasm to make that happen.

"Don't count on any money," I said gloomily. "Matthew's daughter-in-law was being pretty noisy about how she was the only family member left because his sister and son had both died. It sounded as though she expected to inherit as remaining next-of-kin."

I saw Paul give a couple of non-committal nods. "I remember the sister dying. Kidney failure, Matthew said. Nothing suspicious, and she must have been close to eighty. The son though..." He rubbed his chin as he concentrated on the road ahead. "James – always called Jazzy for some reason. A lot younger than Matthew. Iona told me he had some sort of back-country accident a few years ago. Less than forty when it happened. Mountain running? Orienteering? Training for the Coast-to-Coast event? A long way from civilization anyway, and I think that was the main problem. He might have survived if they'd found him earlier."

"Euw. Poor man."

"Sorry," Paul added. "Not the sort of thing you need to hear after what you found earlier today."

I shook my head to show I wasn't too bothered. "But hang on – someone called Jazzy ran the marathon for New Zealand at one of the Olympic Games. It was probably him."

"Don't remember," Paul said. "But it would have been well before I arrived here."

"That's a lot of dead family," I mused. "Wife, sister, his

son, and now Matthew himself. You don't think someone's been systematically bumping them off?"

"Merry!" Paul exclaimed, suddenly all attention. He swiveled toward me, the whites of his eyes shining, even in the darkness of the car.

"Only idle speculation," I added hastily.

It was possibly a good thing we reached The Burkeville a few seconds later because my suggestion had been enough to reduce Paul to silence. He turned into the already crowded parking area and said nothing more until we were out and approaching the front door. Then he gave me a friendly slap on the shoulder. "Sounds like you've been editing too many murder novels."

"Not a one," I said, bumping him back with my elbow, and relieved he'd got past my crass comment. "Lord Drizzle's memoirs, a children's book about birds, an electrical catalog from someone whose first language is plainly not English."

"Variety anyway," Paul said, opening the door for me. "How do you edit an electrical catalog?"

"I'll tell you in a minute, once we've found a seat."

"Hmm, crowded," he observed as we entered. It helps that he's nice and tall. He peered around and spotted a table for two close to the far wall, then slid an arm around me to steer me in the right direction. On Saturday nights The Burkeville is always busy, but it's rare I've seen anyone give up waiting and leave.

Once again I wondered if Paul and I had a future. That arm felt nice, and we were in public, so he wasn't worrying who saw us. Or was it simply politeness and a chivalrous reaction to protect me from the crowd?

My gaze swiveled straight to John Bonnington, busy pouring drinks at the far end of the bar. He was surrounded as usual by gorgeous females. No doubt admiring the muscles stretching his snug T-shirt, and the tanned skin exposed by his short sleeves, and his pulled-up hair, even at this time of year. It was hard to tear my eyes away, because one glimpse of John and my lips automatically parted, remembering that incendiary fake kiss he'd given me to annoy my ex, Duncan.

Unforgettable. Honestly.

I sighed. John lived too fast for me, and always had too many women looking willing and eager.

Put him out of your mind, Merry, I thought, moving off with Paul.

The aroma of hot fries and sizzling steak wafted deliciously through the air. The Saturday night crowd was already making plenty of noise, and I spotted Bernie and Aroha Karaka, our butcher and his wife, close to where we were heading.

If the place hadn't been so noisy I'd have leaned over and asked how the dogs were doing because they'd adopted the two little white Bichons from my first murder victim.

That sounds terrible, doesn't it? As though I have an endless string of victims instead of only three, but let me tell you – three is plenty. I don't want any more. Anyway, I'm sure the dogs are doing well.

"You're looking very nice tonight, Merry," Paul said as he pulled out a chair for me and I sat. Yes, a low-cut jersey and a view from above are always going to draw compliments with a figure like mine. Voluptuous – there's a good word for it. Much nicer than 'busty' or 'top-heavy'.

"Thank you, Paul," I said, glancing up with my smoky eyes and possibly fluttering my well-mascaraed lashes. "You're looking very smart, too."

Indeed he was. Charcoal slacks, navy blazer, blue and white pin-striped shirt, no tie. He needed a big white yacht to complete the picture. And a swanky cap with gold braid.

Cap'n McCreagh. Just right.

He looked down at me quizzically as he rounded the table. "You're drifting off and imagining things again. What are you thinking about?"

I came back to earth with a thump, and probably a blush as well. "Just picturing you in a hat with braid around the peak. To go with the rather nautical blazer."

"Admiral of the Fleet?" he teased. "I was army, not navy."

Yes, he was. An army chaplain who'd seen terrible things he was still affected by. He took the chair opposite me and gazed around.

"No sign of Erik," I said.

"Off in the States for a few days."

I know my eyebrows must have shot halfway up my forehead. "Heather didn't say anything about that when I saw her earlier today."

"She's in a bit of a flap about him, to be honest. Very keen but seems unsettled. I'm worried about the rumors." Paul held my gaze in a way that made me want to confess things.

A shiver of dread trickled down my spine. "You mean the hit-man stories?" I leaned across the table so I could whisper. "Those files I found in Isobel Crombie's office in the garage last year hinted he and John were both tied up in some sort of Black Ops thing, but do you really think it's possible? I mean – they're nice. Really nice, now I've got to know them better. I can't imagine them assassinating anyone, hiding the evidence, and wafting away like smoke as though nothing's happened."

Now it was Paul's turn to raise his eyebrows. "Not quite what I'd heard," he muttered, following it with a bit of throat-clearing and a doubtful frown. "Who told you that, anyway?"

I picked up my menu and avoided his eyes. "I Googled it. They're called Cleaners."

He stifled a laugh. "Well, they were both military, but much more likely to be covert planning specialists than active operatives, given their ages. Especially living out here."

"Although that might be a good cover for them," I suggested, feeling I should play devil's advocate. "They can whizz off and do their dirty work and come home to disguise themselves as bar and café owners again. And helicopter nature tour organizers."

Paul closed his eyes briefly, then opened them and sharpened his gaze on me. "If it's not murder novels you've been editing, then maybe spy stories? Anyway, what would you like to eat? I'll get us a drink."

"Poor Heather," I said, looking at him briefly and then running a finger down my menu. "Is she really worried?"

He leaned back in his chair. "If there are stories like that floating around I can see why. But no – I don't think that's the problem."

Oh dear. Smoothing over the cracks was needed so he'd stop worrying about his sister. "Good. And anyway Bruce Carver made sure I deleted those strange files from my Cloud folder as soon as he had what he wanted."

Paul laid his menu back on the table. "And thank heavens for that. You don't need any connection to something so shady."

"I haven't heard any rumors." My face was growing hot, even though it had no need to. I'm sure I've been the soul of discretion ever since finding the documents. "People are wondering why they're not 'taking things to the next level' romantically, though," I said, with those silly air quotes like people on TV do.

Although of course they might be, and it's none of my business.

"Red or white?" Paul asked in a resigned tone. He sighed, and rubbed the tip of his nose.

Time to change the subject. "I'll have the grilled, spiced lamb rump please. Medium-rare. And a glass of Merlot."

"Lamb it is," he said, scanning his own menu.

"Go for the fish, Vicar," a nearby gravelly voice said. Brett

Royal from the whale-watch boat rose from the next table and leaned over us. "Fresh caught today. Guaranteed not to be whale." He guffawed at his less than funny joke and then turned his attention to my neckline. He had very beery breath.

"Heard you found another one," he said to my breasts.

Well it wasn't *my* fault Matthew had been sitting there dead! But it was exactly the cue the others at his table needed to begin a noisy discussion.

"Give it a rest, Brett," Paul snapped, rising to his feet and towering over the chunky fisherman. The others fell silent. "How would you feel in her place? Merry's civic-minded enough to go collecting for good causes and it puts her in more locations than you get into at sea. Law of averages, isn't it."

Brett wasn't having that. He stuck his chin out. "Three times though, Vicar," he bellowed. "Three dead bodies. It's not natural." He swayed on his feet, and then swayed a lot further. John Bonnington had slid out from behind the bar, made his way swiftly across the room, wrapped one arm across Brett's throat, and used the other to bend the boat-owner's wrist into what looked like a very uncomfortable position.

"All done here?" John suggested in a friendly drawl. "You and your mates have been drinking since the footie finished so maybe you'll be nice enough to free up the table for someone else now?"

One against five. I saw Paul stand up straighter, watchful

as a cat in case he needed to join the fray. There was general masculine bluster from Brett's mates, but John's quiet suggestion, the obvious power in his long muscular arms, and his steely glare, had them shuffling to their feet and shambling out within thirty seconds. Plainly they weren't willing to risk being banned in future.

"Who's your driver?" he called after them. Bugsy Royal raised his hand and kept walking. Bugsy is a fitness fanatic and had probably been on something pretty innocuous for the last few hours because John nodded, gave him a thumbs-up, and added, "Thank you gentlemen," as the troop left.

The excitement was over – but Brett's noisy claim about 'finding another one' had set up a huge buzz of conversation from which the words 'Boatman' and 'shot' and 'dead' were plainly audible. The local gossip grapevine was alive and well.

John stood beside the vacated table, rubbed his hands together, and glanced around his customers. "Anyone else thinking of giving Merry hell?" he invited in a benign tone.

Eyes returned to plates, forks prodded fries, and conversation fell to furtive murmurs.

"Like to order now, Vicar?" he suggested with a grin.

They approached the bar together, my two tall men who were such polar opposites. I bowed my head to avoid the stares, and then thought, 'Well darn, it was hardly my fault!'

I took a deep breath, found the friendly gaze of Bernie Karaka, and called across to him, "Only two, actually. Erik and Heather were with me when we spotted poor David Haldane from the helicopter."

"That's my girl – you tell 'em," Bernie replied, which was possibly unwise with his wife right beside him.

Aroha Karaka sent me an equally toothy grin, though. "Us girls gotta stick up for ourselves, eh!" she exclaimed.

I nodded enthusiastically. "Dogs doing well?" I asked.

She nodded back. "Little sweeties. I got them new coats for the winter."

I waited for the 'pink and blue'.

"Pink and blue," she said. "To match their bed."

Yes, I'd seen the sugar-sweet scene inside the French doors at the front of their house when I'd been dog-walking homeless hounds for Lurline from the animal shelter. "They've got a great spot there," I said to Aroha. "Nice sun and a good view."

I was saved from further pleasantries by Paul's return. He carried two big wine goblets, one half-filled with red and one with white. "Merlot for milady," he said, setting it down in front of me. "You okay?"

"After that?" I tilted my head in the direction of Brett Royal's table which was already being claimed by several of the young women I'd seen fawning over John at the bar. "Never better." I leaned closer to Paul as soon as he sat down. "He's scary, isn't he? Maybe he really *is* one of those Black Oppers?" Then I remembered the plunging neckline of my jersey and straightened up again.

Paul raised his glass to me. The corners of his mouth

quirked. He'd definitely had an eyeful. Or a bra-full. "To a pleasant evening," he said. "And a speedy resolution to Matthew's death."

"Yes please," I begged. "Poor Matthew – I still can't imagine why anyone wanted him dead."

The girl whose chair now backed onto mine swiveled around and demanded, round-eyed, "Did you really find him? That must have been terrible."

I'm sure she'd already had too much to drink if she was prepared to ask a complete stranger something so direct and devastating.

I send her a prim nod.

One of the others joined in with, "Really awful."

"He probably deserved it," a third young woman muttered. "No-one would get murdered like that unless it was personal."

Paul sat up straighter and sent her a 'what the heck?' stare. Then he leaned closer to her. "And how was that?" he asked quietly. I was itching to know, too.

The third floozie tossed her abundant hair and simpered at him. I'm sure she had no idea who he was.

The table erupted into giggles and loud shushing noises. Yes, they'd had too much to drink, all right. I hoped they were getting a cab or an Uber home.

The hair-tosser edged nearer to Paul and whispered, "Pinged with an arrow."

The shushing noises grew more urgent.

"Be quiet, Mel," a blonde with a loud voice snapped.

"Keep your mouth shut," one of the others hissed.

"Gray said not to tell," someone else added, glancing sideways at the friend next to her. All the comments ran together in an urgent muttered chorus.

Pinged? It was a lot more than 'pinged'. And *who'd* said not to tell? Why not?

This sounded like important information. As an occasional accomplice of Detective Sergeant Bruce Carver I heard duty calling me, loud and clear.

I dug my phone out of my bag, set it on my lap where no-one else could see it, and texted him. GIRLS AT THE B/VILLE KNOW ABOUT ARROW. SHOULD THEY? There – if he wanted to follow up, it was over to him.

I glanced at the group again. Goodness, they were out of place here. More hair than a wig boutique, and more sparkles than a ballroom dancing contest. Where had they come from? Maybe they were on their way home from a wedding? Or a beauty pageant?

Paul raised his brows at the 'pinged' woman and leaned even closer to her. I won't pretend I was happy about that. "You mean the Robin Hood type of bow and arrow?" he murmured. "That's barbaric."

She nodded. "I *know*," she purred – practically in his ear. "Terrible. I didn't believe it at first." She raised her fancy-looking green cocktail and took a gulp. "They're only saying 'shot' on the radio," she added.

"Shut up, Mel," the loud blonde snapped again, taking her arm and trying to pull her away from Paul.

I wondered how long before Brucie would notice my text, and whether he and Marian Wick were still on duty at this time of night. If he wanted to come and interview them it would take a while to get here. I'd never seen the group before so could hardly start grilling them for details, but a cunning scheme had occurred to me. I deliberately ignored the girl fawning over Paul and smiled at one of the others. "Have you been to a wedding?" I asked. "You're all looking fantastic. I wish I could ever get my hair to go like yours."

She shook her head. "Not a wedding. A party tonight. The guys are collecting us here."

"Turn around a bit?" I pretended to be inspecting her up-do and the luxuriant cascade at the back. "Can I take a photo for reference? I'd love to try that style with mine."

"Yeah, no probs," my new friend said, obligingly twisting this way and that as I ignored her hair, framed the group up on my screen, and shot three of them together. I thought she might want a look, so started going for a close-up as well, but right at that moment several young men swaggered through the doorway.

"Party-party-party!" the girl named Mel exclaimed, deserting Paul as quickly as she'd snuggled up to him. They all upended their fancy cocktail glasses, gulped down their drinks, and pushed back their chairs.

Talk about the nick of time. At least I could let Bruce Carver know what some of them looked like now, and the name of one. I glanced at Paul and muttered, "Do you think you could get me a vehicle description?"

He narrowed his eyes. The young women were on their way out now, teetering on their skyscraper heels and pulling their tight little skirts straight, so I flashed my phone screen with the text at him. "Ah," he said. "Not just a pretty face, are you?"

I tried not to look pleased at that as he rose and followed them to the parking lot. Probably enjoying their tight little skirts.

11

ENDLESS INTERRUPTIONS

WHEN PAUL RETURNED with details of a car and a double-cab pickup truck, I decided to send them on to DS Carver, along with my photo and the name Mel. It was pretty pointless for him to trail out to Burkeville with no-one to interrogate when he arrived.

Voice or text? If he had questions then a call was better. I took another sip of Merlot to fortify myself and selected his name from my contacts list. Then I backed myself into a corner and cupped my hand over my mouth so my voice wouldn't carry far. I definitely didn't want anyone hearing what I was saying and assuming I was a police informer.

"Ms Summerfield," he grated. Not very welcoming!

I dared myself to reply 'Hi Bruce', and then said, "Detective. Just an update on that group."

"I'm sorry – what? Can you speak up?"

Ah... not really the plan!

"I'm trying to keep this confidential," I explained. "I can't speak much louder."

"Yes-yes."

Saying it twice the way he does always makes me grin to myself. Whether he wants it to sound extra urgent, or he hopes it will hurry me up, I've no idea.

I took a furtive glance around. No-one seemed to be listening to me. "I presume you got my text, but they've gone," I said. "I took a photo for you, and one of them is called Mel. I thought it was a bit suspicious they knew about the arrow."

"The what?" He cleared his throat.

"The arrow."

He got the point. "Ah. Definitely. Definitely. The precise cause of death hasn't been supplied to the media, so you've done absolutely the right thing. But you say they've left?"

"Gone to a party," I muttered. I took another sip of Merlot. "I'll send the photo to you in case it's any help for ID. And we have details of two vehicles they're in. I'll get those to you, too, and you'll have everything in one place."

"We?" he asked. And then plainly thought better of starting a long conversation. "Thank you Ms Summerfield." Boy, there was a world of weariness in his voice.

Before he disconnected I asked quickly, "Have you broken through all those newspapers yet?"

I didn't expect he'd answer, but maybe in return for the intel I was providing he said, "Making good progress. We've already forced open a couple of the doors off the hallway, and should have the others clearer by morning."

"Are the rooms full of stuff, too?"

A loud sigh followed my query. "So stuffed with 'stuff', it's going to take days."

"Right," I agreed, sensing I'd probably asked enough. "Stand by for the photo and the vehicle details."

I sat again, and turned to Paul. "Can you send me your info? I'll pass it on with the photo."

We probably looked like a couple of teenagers with our heads down, tapping away, but once things had gone through we were finally able to relax. Paul raised his glass to me and smiled. "You're looking wonderful tonight, Merry. Not like a woman who had such a shocking fright earlier today."

I raised mine in return. "Well, I was worried I *might* look the worse for wear because of it, so I made an effort for you." There – let him make of that what he liked!

"It certainly worked." His dark eyes regarded me with appreciation, which more than compensated for him getting so up-close-and-personal with tarty Mel Hair-and-Sequins.

"Lovely wine," I said, taking a sip and licking my bottom lip in case I'd left a drip of it there. I was pretty sure I hadn't, but Paul's gaze followed the tip of my tongue in a most satisfactory manner.

"It's good to see you again," he murmured. "Properly, I mean. Not just bumping into you at Iona's or passing you in the street."

I gave a slow nod, and we sat there sipping in comfortable silence. After a few minutes he raised his glass in my direction and I raised mine back. We clinked them together before each taking another sip of wine. It felt like a pledge. Did this mean he felt he'd finally got past the worst of his PTSD and was prepared to give me a whirl?

Right at the wrong moment our server arrived at the table, arms extended, and bounty balanced on big white plates. Sizzling lamb rump for me and a gleaming slab of crispy skinned salmon for Paul. I'd never claim the Burkeville is the epitome of fine dining, but their portions are generous, their salads are delicious, their bread is to die for, and their fries set new standards in crispy heaven.

Flirtation could wait, but I couldn't. I set down my glass, picked up my knife and fork, and prepared to be wowed. After the day I'd had, I deserved it.

I thought some more about the possibility of Paul and I together as I chomped and chewed and savored and swallowed. Well, if he was game, so was I, but this was no place for romance.

First, our server paused on the way back from delivering someone else's food and announced, "No wonder you felt like a night away from Drizzle Bay after finding another body." And then, when Paul cleared his throat meaningfully, added, "Tropical fruit cheesecake's really good tonight."

The table the girls had vacated was claimed by Mr and Mrs Patel from the Mini Mart and their three lively children. "Our twelfth wedding anniversary, isn't it!" Raina Patel exclaimed happily and loudly, golden embroidery on her sari flashing, and all her best jewelry on display. Because she'd sold me the jumbo bag of Fortune Kitty, she added, "You found homes for any of poor dead Matthew Boatman's cats yet?"

The volume of the conversation around us rose as the level of the drinks fell, and John's plea 'not to give Merry hell' was soon ignored.

"I heard they used a pistol," an unknown man said to me as he paused by our table. "Do they think it was that chap who always wears the cowboy boots?"

"Shush, Tom," his wife admonished. "You can't make accusations like that in public."

"Or in private," Paul grated, giving him a glare that moved them on.

"Had to be a hunting rifle," one of Lord Drizzle's farmhands claimed, plainly hoping for gossip as he and his wife slowed beside us. "Will they be interviewing everyone from the Gun Club, Vicar?"

Paul shook his head and said more kindly, "How would I know about that, George? You need to ask Detective Sergeant Carver."

And then, horror of horrors, only minutes later, the woman through the hedge from Matthew's house dragged her other half across to us as though she knew me well, and said in a piercing voice, "It's a wonder we weren't murdered too, living right next door to Mr Boatman, as we do. It could easily have been us!" She gazed around, hand clasped against her chest, drawing as much attention to herself as possible, and I'm sure thoroughly embarrassing her poor husband.

They were the last interruption Paul could take. He checked my plate and made sure I'd finished my main course. "Right!" he growled. "So much for a quiet night out. Grab your bag, Merry. I'll collect some of that cheesecake to go, and we'll get out of this madhouse."

The thing about being a vicar is that your voice can be pitched to carry quite a long distance for sermons. The other diners all tilted away like the Red Sea parting for Moses and we made our way unhindered across to the bar. John either has fantastic hearing or he can read minds as one of his superpowers because he said, "Cheesecake won't be a moment," as he accepted Paul's credit card. He sent me a wink as we left, and murmured, "Don't do anything I wouldn't."

Well, really!

What wouldn't he do? Not much, in my opinion...

———

WHEN PAUL BRAKED to a halt outside the Summerfield residence, I leaned encouragingly in his direction and he followed suit and – surprise, surprise – we shared a very nice kiss. In case you're wondering, yes there was gentle moaning and heavy breathing, and his fingers winding and threading through my long blonde tresses, and me smoothing my palm up over his close-shaven face and into his thick dark hair. Possibly to ensure he stayed there for longer.

Then Graham came bursting out of the house with Manny and Dan on their leads, all whistles and barks and a big slam of the front door as he departed, and I just *knew* he was trying to spoil the moment. Maybe to ensure his willing cook and housekeeper stayed living at home for the foreseeable future.

I could have killed him.

I pulled away from Paul and muttered, "Hold that thought."

He gave a rueful chuckle and patted my shoulder. "Big brother warning me off, is he?"

I huffed with indignation. "It's none of his business. He has Susan Hammond when he can be bothered, and I don't interfere with that arrangement."

Paul's fingers stroked up and down my neck. "Susan Hammond who's Betty McGyver's sister?" he asked before lifting his hand away.

"Is she?" I hadn't known that. "Does she live with Betty out at Horse Heaven in Old Bay Road?"

"No idea. But Graham's sweet on her?"

'Sweet on her' was the understatement of the year. How polite of Paul to describe it like that. Graham and Susan had engaged in passionate overnighters for a couple of years now, from which he'd return looking rumpled and relaxed – and then there'd be no more for a while. Was it because he didn't want to embarrass me by bringing her back to the old family home? Or was it because she lived with the formidable Betty and they didn't want her to know what was going on?

And then a thunderbolt hit me. Was it possible Graham was not so much 'warning Paul off' as giving us a bit of privacy by taking his dogs for a walk surprisingly late at night?

"Come on," I said, pushing my door open and considering that as an alternative. "Let's enjoy that cheesecake – and I've got some sachets of really good German drinking chocolate seeing we missed our coffee." I reached over and patted his hand. "Or tea, if you'd rather," I offered, remembering what he mostly drank.

And that's how Graham found us when he returned some time later. Sitting close together on the sofa, empty cups and cheesecake plates on the coffee table in front of us, me with no lipstick, Paul with some on his collar, and probably each of us with dopey grins.

Shame on you if you're thinking anything more than a cuddle happened. He's a vicar, he has a reputation to uphold, and we'll be feeling our way very carefully into this thing – if indeed it turns out to be 'a thing'.

12

A NOT-SO-YUMMY MUMMY

NEXT MORNING I left home while Graham was still in the shower and arrived bright and early to find 17 Paradise Road a hive of quiet efficiency. The gate was chocked open so the newspaper carriers could bring their carefully checked armloads out to the dumpster. No-one was guarding the front door. No nosy neighbors intruded, and there was no sign of Jude Boatman and her flashy motorcycle.

I carried my big bag of Fortune Kitty up the front path and around to the greenhouse, nodding to anyone who glanced at me. Someone must have mentioned what was happening with the cats because people simply responded with nods of their own. I noted the padlock on the back door of the garage was locked again. The front was still undisturbed. Darn – no chance to check out the car (or cars). And the curtains still covered all the windows, so plainly no-one had made it far enough into any of the crowded rooms to pull them aside.

My lazy little poppets were still in bed – and looking pretty cute, I have to admit. The low sun flooded Feline HQ with a golden glow, but it took only one keen furry ear to hear the rustle of the kibble and they were all attention. I pushed the screeching door aside so I could get through, and a chorus of encouraging mewing and purring filled the formerly quiet air.

"All right. Hang on. Wait a minute," I told them, trying not to step on paws or tails. Not a single piece of kibble graced the big terracotta saucer. Was I feeding them enough? I tipped out a generous stream of it, which bounced off ears and noses, and missed the saucer entirely sometimes. I had no worries they'd find it and clean it up, though.

Then I stood back and watched. Siam was gone of course. Peanut was still there, so it looked as though Poppy Waitomo would get her birthday gift. Tubby Fifty was surprisingly polite, given that his bulbous body could probably push anyone else out of the way with the merest nudge. Once again old Skinnyblack had taken up position paws-in-plate and the others were diving under his or her saggy belly to grab their breakfast. Yes, the other black cat definitely only had one eye, poor thing, but seemed to be fending for itself perfectly well. The name Onesie came to mind – or was that too cruel?

Why was there now someone new in the crew? A rangy white animal with a couple of disconcerting patches of black and ginger. A trespasser. Word had obviously sped around the feline network there was free food and lodging available at 17 Paradise Road. I wanted fewer cats, not more of them. And wasn't there supposed to be a third black one?

"Oi! Whiteguy!" I tried. "Get out of here." I bent down and gave its tail a small tug and got a lightning fast swat from a claw-tipped paw for my temerity. It missed me, but it got the plastic bag. Fortune Kitty streamed down from the new hole in the base and I grabbed at it like the little Dutch boy trying to stem the flow of water from the hole in the dyke. Really – how rude!

I backed away and returned the Fortune Kitty to the car – positioning it so no more could escape. Then I returned to Feline HQ and topped up the water containers, feeling a little mean it wasn't milk. Too much luxury shouldn't be provided though or they'd never move out.

I was wandering back along the front path – slowly and quietly, so I could do as much eavesdropping as possible – when a piercing and unearthly scream issued through the open doorway, accompanied by the noise of clumsy crashing around. I froze on the spot.

It was a female voice. Panicked and shocked. And then I made out the words, "She's been mummified! Get Bruce."

That had to be Marian Wick doing the screaming because I doubted anyone else would dare to refer to the Detective Sergeant as 'Bruce'."

Who had been mummified? Surely not Mrs Boatman

who'd died years ago, and for whom Graham had prepared divorce papers which were never needed?

Drawn like a bee to nectar, I trotted across to the front door – right in time to be cannoned into by Detective Wick as she hurtled out on her long legs. We collapsed into a heap on the lawn, each of us gasping and exclaiming for different reasons.

"Mrs Boatman?" I squeaked, with the air knocked out of me.

"Mmm," she confirmed, swallowing hard and slapping a hand over her mouth.

"What...?" I asked, getting an arm free, and hoping she wasn't going to be sick on me.

"Dead for years," she gasped. "It's set up like a weird shrine in there. No wonder he pulled the curtains across."

Bruce Carver thundered along the timber-floored hallway and out into the front yard. "Marian?" he asked. "What the...?"

"I'll be okay," she assured him, panting up at him and then looking down at me. "Just give me a mo. Wasn't expecting that."

The rest of the Police team had gathered around, waiting expectantly for information.

"What happened?" I asked from underneath her. She was quite bony. I'd definitely be nicer to cuddle.

She scrunched her eyes closed as though trying to un-see whatever she'd just found. After taking a deep breath, she told us all, "We got enough rubbish moved that I could get into the front room, being the thinnest one here..."

Ow – she had very sharp hips.

"I didn't see that coming, I can tell you," she mumbled as she finally levered herself off me.

I sat up and rubbed my throbbing ankle – possibly kicked by one of her shoes as she came bursting out of the house.

"And I wormed my way in as far as the window to get the curtains opened," she continued, "because the light bulb must have blown years ago."

"Black as the Ace of Spades in there," Bruce Carver said to no-one in particular. "Do you need to sit down, Marian?"

Noooo... I begged silently. I wanted to hear the rest.

"I'm okay," she said, taking a couple of steps so she could lean on the door-frame. "But... yes... once I dragged one of the curtains aside, I saw what was around the back of all the piles of rubbish, where we couldn't see with the torches from the front. There's a sofa with a kind of framework on top, and a net. I managed to grab a corner of the net and pull it away – and there she was. Or what's left of her, anyway."

"A shrine?" Bruce Carver asked.

She shuddered. "A cross, and big vases of dusty artificial roses and so on. I only got a glimpse before I bolted out."

"I don't blame you," I said, accepting the hand of a large policeman who hauled me up to lean on the other side of the doorframe. I nodded my thanks and turned back to her.

"Was it a mosquito net to keep the flies off her? They lived in Africa at one stage. A long time ago."

"How do you know that?" Bruce Carver demanded as someone produced two bottles of water and handed them to me and my new friend, Marian.

I couldn't help wishing it was a stiff gin as I unscrewed the cap. "My brother told me. Yesterday, when I got home. He'd been out golfing."

"Yes-yes. And?"

I took a swig of water. "I told him I'd found poor old Mr Boatman dead in the kitchen, and he mentioned them as past clients. He said they were going to divorce but she died before they could. You should ask him about dates."

Bruce Carver scratched his inadequate goatee and squinted at me.

Then I had a better thought. "Jim Drizzle knows a lot more. I bumped into him on the beach, and he said... well... he said Mr Boatman dragged Mrs Boatman off to Africa while she was pregnant. He disapproved."

Marian Wick and Bruce Carver both shook their heads. "I hope you're not thinking of solving this murder, too," he said.

"It was a walk on the beach," I protested. "And I haven't solved any of them, really. Just been in the right places at the wrong times." I thought about that for a moment. "Or the wrong places at the right times, I suppose." The rest of the Police team was trying not to snigger. I rolled my eyes and drank some more water, determined to say nothing else if that's the way he was going to react to my useful information. "Zimbabwe!" I exclaimed as I suddenly recalled Jim's saying it. "That's where they went."

"*Thank* you Ms Summerfield," Bruce Carver said, sounding not the least bit thankful. He turned away from me and gazed into the house. "So I'll need more of a passageway cleared out so we can reach the second deceased," he instructed, gesturing his team back in. "Sounded like you bashed your way out?" he suggested to Marian Wick.

"Definitely lost my cool there for a moment," she agreed.

"Anyone would have," I said in a consoling tone.

This brought a razor-sharp glare from Bruce Carver before he turned away to chivvy his helpers into further action.

Oh well. That was that for now. I wondered how long before they'd make an official announcement.

I needed to tell Paul. He was a good bet because he wouldn't tell anyone else. And for sure he'd want to do some sort of blessing or a prayer for poor old Mrs Boatman, although she might not have been all that old at the time she... um... died.

I wonder *how* she died?

———

I DROVE down Paradise Road a short distance, stopped and rubbed my sore ankle, grateful it wasn't my accelerator/brake foot, and phoned him. "Paul – thank you so much for the meal last night."

I heard his soft laugh. "Bit of a fiasco, really. With all those comments from the other diners. I should have expected that and steered clear of The Burkeville."

I folded the rear-view mirror down and checked my appearance after my unexpected tumble onto Matthew's front lawn. Thank heavens we'd missed the concrete path. "I thoroughly enjoyed the good food and the good company across the table, though. But could we meet for a chat?"

I heard surprise in his tone as he asked, "Everything okay?"

Lying only a little, I said, "Almost. Just a rather strange thing I need to tell you face to face. Is Heather there? It won't matter if she is."

"Gone to The Café. Probably up to her elbows in flour by now."

"But are *you* busy?"

"Nothing happening until a while later. What's wrong, Merry?"

"See you in five minutes," I said, and disconnected.

I arrived in four, and found him already waiting by the front of the Vicarage, weight on one leg, with his other ankle crossed languidly over it as he leaned back on the fence trying not to look anxious. He could have been a male model in his close-fitting black running trousers and long-sleeved grey tank. I knew he was the basketball coach for Burkeville

Secondary School's large and troublesome senior boys, and had a nice bod, but hmmm....

He immediately stood up straighter as I pulled in beside him. For sure there was a blush climbing up my neck and cheeks. My cat-feeding jeans and warm jersey (possibly with mud and grass-stains now) showed me off to much less advantage than the unexpectedly streamlined clothing he was wearing. Hot vicar. Looking hotter to me every day.

A second or two later he was opening my door. I stepped out, a bit flustered, and said, "Sorry about this. I didn't mean to panic you. There's nothing either of us can do to reverse the situation." I glanced up the road and gave a brief wave to Drizzle Bay's resident handyman, Jasper Hornbeam, who was measuring something for the fence at old Mrs Winslow's.

Paul opened the gate and waited until I'd passed through. Then he walked ahead of me up the short front path, glancing over his shoulder to make sure I was following. "You've got me even more worried now," he said. "Reverse *what* situation exactly?"

The front door wasn't closed. He pushed it with his hand and it swung open. Somehow the furnishings looked entirely right for a debonair Englishman. Polished hardwood floors, a long, patterned carpet runner leading right up the hallway in the center of the house, paintings of boats, biblical scenes, and possibly the River Nile in dark frames, and brass candlesticks on the mantelpiece of the sunny room he led me through to. I'd been there before to visit Heather, and not taken much notice; it had felt half holy and half old-fashioned. Now I saw it through different eyes. Classy and timeless.

Before I could say another word he pulled me close, tilted my face up, and gave me a kiss that would have shocked Saint Agatha's congregation, had they seen it. It made my toes curl and my eyelids flutter closed, and I heard someone groan. I suspect it was me.

"Just in case that's the situation you were thinking of reversing?" he asked in a tight voice as he drew away.

"No," I protested. "Definitely not." I probably gazed at him open-mouthed until I collected my wits again. "It's to do with Matthew Boatman."

He sent me a pleased and possibly relieved grin. "Tea? I put the water on to boil as soon as you phoned."

I nodded, crossing to the windows and gazing out at the ocean as I recovered from our scorching and unexpected kiss. Phew. And holy moly. And quite a lot of other things along those lines.

The house fronted right onto the beach and was set in a grove of *pohutukawa* trees. The side rooms had to be quite shady, but here the sun and the view were both glorious.

I heard the electric kettle coming to a rolling boil again so I turned and pulled out a chair from the gleaming oak table Paul had already set with cups and saucers. He joined me a few moments later with a teapot that matched the cups, and sat it on a cork mat.

I ran my forefinger over the shiny old timber and plunged ahead. "Matthew Boatman had a wife," I began.

Paul gave a slow nod. "Never met her. Dead and buried many years ago."

How was I going to explain this in any way that wasn't totally offensive to a religious man? "Um, well, not entirely, it seems."

He tilted his head a little and I realized part of the reason he looked so casual and sporty this morning was because he wasn't wearing his white dog collar.

I swallowed. "Dead for sure," I agreed, and hurried on. "But I've just been to feed the cats and I'm afraid they found her inside the house. Her body, I mean. In a kind of shrine, Marian Wick said."

Paul's dark brows snapped together and he stared at me. "But..."

"Under a mosquito net in the front sitting room." I closed my eyes for a few seconds, and opened them again to find him still staring straight at me. "So that explains why all the curtains were constantly drawn. He didn't want anyone to see in. I'll bet he never invited anyone inside. Only had those cats for company."

"In a *shrine?*" Paul repeated, sharpening his gaze even further.

"According to Marian Wick she's laid out peacefully on a sofa with a cross and vases of artificial flowers. And kind of mummified, so she must have been there for years. She needs some prayers, Paul. I thought you'd want to know."

He bowed his head and I saw his lips move in a private incantation. Then he looked up at me again. "Thank you Merry. She does. And it would be my privilege to arrange a proper burial service for her and try to put things as right as possible."

"It's only just happened. Literally minutes ago." I shook myself like a wet dog, probably now partly in shock as it started to sink in. My body count had just gone up to four. I was jinxed. Doomed. Plagued by constant death.

"Do you want my phone?" I asked in a shaky voice. "In case you don't have Bruce Carver's number?" I rooted around in my bag for it.

Paul could see I was rattled. He said quietly, "Pull up your contacts and I'll put his number into mine."

It seemed there was just room inside those stretchy skin-tight sports pants to accommodate a phone because he dug it out and set it on the table beside the tea things.

13

TEA AND SYMPATHY

"Maybe a double funeral?" I whispered. "Matthew and his wife together? Although I suppose someone in the family would have to okay that."

He breathed out a long, slow sigh. "From the comments Matthew let slip at the Seniors Afternoons there was no-one left."

"There's his daughter-in-law," I said. "From Rotorua. She turned up on a motor cycle yesterday, looking pretty tough. A bulky black jacket. Not leather, but whatever they wear these days. Is it Kevlar?"

He shook his head. "Under the top fabric, maybe. That's the stuff in bullet-proof vests." And of course he'd know that because of being a chaplain in Afghanistan. I immediately felt stupid.

"But Matthew never mentioned her," he added. "How on earth do you know about her?"

I shrugged, picturing the vivid scene from the previous afternoon. "She arrived at the house because she'd seen a tweet or something about the police being there. She expected Bruce Carver to let her in. He told her in no uncertain terms it was an active crime scene and to keep clear. I thought I told you."

I was sure I had – on the way to The Burkeville – but maybe there were other things on Paul's mind last evening. Things like me. Us.

Hmmm...

He rubbed his chin. Deliciously bristly, now I looked more closely. How had I not felt that when he'd kissed me?

"Do you know her name?" he asked.

"Jude Boatman. Judith? You could ask Bob Burgess at the Courier. She gave her card to the WPC guarding the gate and flounced off when she was refused entry, and then Bob started chatting up the WPC – whose name is Bess Moody, by the way – and I kind of overheard them saying Rotorua because he Googled her."

A reluctant grin tweaked at the corners of Paul's mouth. "Not much gets past you, does it?"

"I've no idea why she's here from Rotorua, though. Is it suspicious timing? Was she planning to kill Matthew? And if so, what for?"

Paul raised an eyebrow, gave the teapot a swirl, and poured us each a cup of pale steaming tea. "I doubt she'd make herself so visible in that case."

Yes, he was right. "I suppose." I sniffed at the rising steam.

"Earl Grey. Is that all right for you?"

"Fine, Paul. Thank you."

He gnawed his bottom lip for a few seconds. "Poor old girl – I wonder how she died? Maybe Matthew was so heart-broken he couldn't bear to be without her?"

I raised a brow. "Or maybe he killed her – accidentally or on purpose – and didn't want to own up and go to jail for it?"

Paul sighed, took a sip of his tea, pursed his lips when he found it too hot, and put his cup down again. "I can't imagine that. He's the soul of propriety."

"Not according to Jim Drizzle who disapproves of him more than somewhat. Matthew used to race Italian cars back when Jim used to race motor cycles. Not that he exactly criticized that – pot/kettle and so on – but he insisted his wife went to live in Africa when she was pregnant and unwell."

"Matthew did? Good grief..."

"Yes, not all sweetness and light, after all. But a long time ago now."

Paul drew his phone closer. "I'll call Bruce Carver and offer my services."

I rose and walked to the French doors with their view of the beach, trying to avoid hearing the details and giving him some privacy for his chat. Our parents' joint funeral wasn't so far in the past, and that'll never leave my mind, so I stared out at the sea and the wheeling seagulls, sipping my fragrant, too-hot tea with caution, and filling in a few minutes that way.

Once he'd finished I turned around again and sat. "All under control?"

"Probably far from, but a start, anyway."

"You look quite different like that," I said without meaning to. "In sports clothes, I mean."

Paul checked his watch. "I haven't started work for the day yet, but I like to keep fit." He gave me a gentle smile. "It doesn't seem quite dignified to go out pounding the streets in my position, Merry. Have you any idea what time it is?"

A glance at my watch showed barely eight-thirty. Never! Had I really been so eager to get to Paradise Road that I'd bolted out super-early? I'd probably arrived not long after 8 o'clock, and without breakfast. My stomach gave a noisy rumble to confirm that situation.

"I hope I'm not here too soon for you. Didn't mean to interrupt your morning routine."

His smile grew broader. "Well, it *is* Sunday. In my line of work I have a bit to do, but not until later."

I gasped so suddenly I almost coughed. I'd totally forgotten what day it was. I lurched up out of my chair.

He held up a hand. "Sit down, Merry! I'd have kicked you out earlier if it was a problem. Early Communion at Totara Flat doesn't happen until the milking's done and they've cleaned up on the dairy farms there. Family Service is back here at Saint Agatha's at eleven-thirty. Evensong's along at the Burkeville Chapel this evening, seeing it's the first Sunday of the month."

He plucked the stretchy T-shirt away from his chest and let it snap back into place. "Heather and I have a cross-trainer in the corner bedroom, and that's why you found me like... this."

I drew a sharp breath and tried to cover it with a question. "Okay then. But I wonder where Jude Boatman is now? If she's come down from Rotorua on that motorbike she must be staying somewhere."

"Drink your tea," Paul said, taking a sip of his. "Try and forget about the situation. Let the police sort it out."

I nodded like a bobble-headed dog, but I knew my brain wasn't likely to calm down any time soon.

———

HOWEVER, speak of the devil!

I left the vicarage about twenty minutes later so Paul could have a shower and make himself look clerical. I was hoping Iona had The Café opened by then. Blueberry pancakes really appealed for breakfast, so I pulled up beside a muddy pick-up truck with a couple of sheepdogs in the back and moseyed on in. The first thing I saw, lit up like a bonfire in a beam of bright sunshine, was Jude Boatman's spectacular red hair.

In for a penny, in for a pound, so I approached her table and said, "Hello. It's me from yesterday. The cats. Are you okay after that horrible shock?"

She looked a lot more approachable out of her motor

cycle gear. Quite smart, in fact. In jeans again, but this time teamed with a pink jersey that had a high polo collar. It shouldn't have worked with her hair, but somehow it did. She jumped a bit – miles away in her thoughts, I suppose.

"Merry Summerfield," I said. And then added, more softly, "I found him. Can I join you, or would you rather be alone?"

"No, no, by all means," she said in her upmarket voice. "You might be able to shed a bit more light."

Okay, that was progress. "I'll order something to eat." I trotted across to the counter and grinned at Iona's raised eyebrows.

"You're early," she said. "What's up?"

"I'm feeding Matthew Boatman's cats. Six of them. That's why I wanted the plastic containers yesterday." I peered up at the chalkboard menu on the wall. "Thanks for them – they worked fine. Blueberry pancakes please. Yoghurt on the side."

"And your usual?" she said, taking a coffee cup from the stack.

"Absolutely." I handed over my card, and added quietly, "That's his daughter-in-law, poor thing."

You always get more from Iona if you're prepared to trade gossip, and on this occasion she muttered, "She was very fond of him."

Was she indeed? Until yesterday I hadn't known she existed, but I suppose she could have been zooming up and down Paradise Road every fortnight to visit him, incognito inside her crash helmet, and I'd never have had a clue.

But no – she wouldn't have let him live in all that mess if she was 'very fond' of him...

"Did she tell you that?" I asked.

Iona leaned closer. "No – Matthew did, quite a while ago. He had more time for her than he did for his good-for-nothing spendthrift son."

Ooops. Not the marathon runner, surely? The national hero who'd died a tragic early death? "Jazzy?" I asked. "Er – James?"

"That was him." Further comments were drowned out by the coffee-making noises, and then she handed the steaming cup over, swiftly processed my card, and said, "Won't be long."

I carried it back to Jude's table, and sat. I was itching to tell her about her long-dead mother-in-law of course but knew that wasn't my business. And anyway, it might have distracted her too much from the current discussion I wanted to have.

She beat me to it with a question. "Why is it you who's feeding the cats?"

I tipped some sugar into my coffee. "I was collecting for the Red Cross yesterday and thought it was odd his door was open but he wasn't answering it –"

"So you knew him?" she interrupted.

"Only to wave to as I walked dogs past his front fence. I'm fond of animals. I sometimes house-sit for people with pets."

It wouldn't be too strong a description to say she was sending me an incinerating glare.

I picked up my teaspoon. "When he didn't come to the door I started worrying he might be ill. I went in and found him." I set the spoon down again. "Wish I hadn't, but at least it got things rolling when I reported it to the police. They asked me to wait there until they arrived." I picked up the spoon again and gave the coffee a stir. "Not to wait inside, obviously. There were several hungry cats hanging around so I offered to feed them to keep them out of the police's way."

She nodded, tight-lipped, and we stared glumly at each other.

I took a sip of my latte. "Did you know Matthew was dead before you arrived?" I asked. Crass of me, but sometimes a direct question cuts through a lot of rubbish.

With only the slightest hesitation she said, "No. Heavens, no! But something strange had happened, and I wanted to check it out."

This made no sense to me but I gave her an encouraging nod.

"His son... James... and I... had a rather odd marriage." It was her turn to tip sugar into her coffee and give it a stir. While she was doing this Iona bustled across with her Eggs Bene and I feared the moment was lost.

"Coming right up," Iona said to me, beetling off again.

"Me and my past husband, too," I said, hoping to get Jude back on track.

She took a sip of coffee and ground some pepper over her eggs. "He was an athlete."

"Matthew was very proud of him," I murmured. Well, I suppose he was. What father wouldn't be proud to have an Olympian for a son?

"I doubt that," Jude snapped. "But he might have spread the idea around to save face." She poked her fork into one of the egg yolks and watched it ooze out, over the smoked salmon and the toast, until it pooled on the plate. "Unfaithful pig," she added, cutting a corner off the toast and dabbing it in the egg.

It seemed best to stay quiet. I did a bit of sympathetic nodding.

She swallowed her mouthful and looked me full in the face again. "We had problems conceiving children, so he went and made someone else pregnant to get a kid." The corners of her mouth turned down.

Bastard! I thought. At least Duncan hadn't done that to me. Or not that I knew about.

The Café was slowly filling up. Families hoping to beat the weekend queue were bustling in, laughing and chatting. It would be hopeless for sharing confidences in a few more minutes.

I sipped my coffee and put my cup down again. "We could just have our breakfast here and then go somewhere quieter to talk, if you like."

She shook her head. "It's freezing outside, even in the sun."

I thought fast. "I meant to the church. Saint Agatha's. It's close and peaceful, and the vicar's a friend of mine. Matthew went to his Seniors Afternoons."

She inserted another mouthful just as Iona arrived with my blueberry pancakes.

"Oopsie," Iona said, shepherding a small girl back in the direction of her mother. Jude's gaze followed the child hungrily and then settled on my pancakes.

"Okay. The church," she agreed, once she'd swallowed. "Those look nice."

"Too nice to have very often."

She grinned, and then added, "You know he died a couple of years ago? Matthew's son?"

I nodded as I started on the first pancake. "Out training, and got lost and injured?"

"Fitting," she said. "At least Grace couldn't have him either, after that."

Ouch. Nasty.

She fell silent, so we ate our breakfasts and drank our coffees while I considered her snarky comments. Then I guided her out through the chaos and headed toward the privacy of the church, knowing it wouldn't be in use until Paul returned to conduct Family Service later in the morning. The narrow garden beds around its foundations frothed with dainty pink and white primulas, planted alternately. He likes his 'grand old lady' to look pretty.

Inside, the sun scattered rubies and emeralds over the pews as it beamed through the big stained-glass window behind the altar, but it was too bright to easily look at. I led Jude across to one side where the Lord and Lady Drizzle windows were. Designed by Lady Zinnia and presented to Saint Agatha's on its centenary. I loved them. Blue sky, green hills, bands of dark trees, and grazing animals. Just right for a country church.

"They're hard old pews," I said. "Sit on a kneeler." I handed her one of the padded squares and took one for myself, then we both bowed our heads for a few moments in recognition of this being a holy place.

Sprays of evergreens and big white arum lilies stood in the vases up the front. A few lemony daffodils brightened the lower part of the arrangements, but we were too far away for their fragrance to reach us. I couldn't help thinking of Isobel Crombie who Paul and I had discovered lying dead in the aisle the year before. She'd been surrounded by flowers and pieces of smashed pottery, and finding her killer had led us into interesting places.

Jude broke into my reflections by turning to me and saying bitterly, "James played me and Grace against each other. He wanted to keep living with me because of his father. He didn't want to be disinherited. He was sure the old boy was worth a heap and he wasn't going to risk missing out. He knew his Dad disapproved of divorce."

But not, apparently, mistresses, although perhaps Matthew had never known about Grace.

I blinked. "Missing out on what? The Italian cars?"

She looked at me blankly. "Did he have more than one?"

"Two I think, and quite expensive."

"The bike's Italian," she murmured. "Ducati. Used to be Jazzy's. Only the best for him."

"So missing out on what, if not the cars?" I asked, trying to get her back on topic.

"Anything he'd brought back from Africa. Anything he'd mined and taken out of the country illegally."

"Really?" I gaped at her. Mild-mannered old Matthew was turning into a real surprise. "You think he smuggled ɜtuff?"

She sniffed. "Would have been pretty easy, back then. A few ounces are worth a bomb if the stones are good. They'd fit in your pocket, wrapped in a handkerchief."

"Goodness," I murmured, remembering she had 'gemologist' on her business card. Presumably she knew what she was talking about.

"*So*," she added suddenly after taking a deep breath. "Jazzy got a child out of Grace when I couldn't give him one. He pretended to his dad that she was ours to keep the old boy sweet. Then he got himself killed and Grace was left holding the baby, so to speak. She didn't want it much and I did. We came to a kind of unofficial child-share arrangement, which left her in the box seat with all the ammo. If I wanted to keep seeing Sasha, I pretty much had to toe Grace's line. Fall in with her plans. Take the crumbs I could get." She pulled her bottom lip in over her teeth and bit down hard on it – maybe to stop the flow of words.

Her yearning expression when Iona had led the little girl

back to her mother in The Café suddenly made sense, and now I was thinking of my dad. 'In the box-seat with all the ammo' was something he used to say. I'll bet Jude's did, too. I warmed a little more toward her. "And where's Sasha now?"

"Spending the weekend at her bestie's home. She's only six. I need to phone and ask if they can keep her another day or two now this has happened."

I left a small silence before I asked, "You said when we were in The Café that something odd had occurred, which is why you came down to Drizzle Bay. What was it?"

Jude pressed her lips together. "Someone – Grace – took the key to Pa-in-law's house off my key-ring. Sasha's little hands couldn't have managed that. Grace denied it of course, but the bundle lives in my handbag – and if I'm home, it's in the lock inside the front door. I don't think she'd have searched my bag, but the front door would have been easy to take it from. His old key had a pretty awful cat-face ornament attached to it that Sasha made at school, so it was easy to spot it was missing."

I nodded to encourage her to keep talking. "But why would she take it?"

Jude sent me a sideways glance that was half annoyance and half embarrassment. "Jazzy used to boast to her that his dad was rich and had gemstones hidden away. Taunting and teasing her. Grace has a strange personality. She's single-minded. You do things her way or they don't happen. She might have thought they'd be easy pickings and finally decided to come and search for them."

I snorted with laughter. "She'll be lucky!"

"Pardon?" Jude demanded at my gleeful comment.

"Well – you've seen inside his house?"

She glared at me, stammered, stopped, and shook her head.

I was going to enjoy this. "He's a total hoarder. The place is stuffed full of rubbish. Have you never seen inside?"

The head-shaking continued, and now she was definitely blushing.

My spidey senses fizzed and tingled. Had she really not known? Odd.

"Maybe that explains something, though," she added quickly. "Jazzy said he didn't bother visiting his father because the old boy liked driving. He turned up often enough that we never felt the need to reciprocate."

"He might have been keeping you all away," I suggested.

"Sounds entirely possible." Then she frowned. "Do you mean Jazzy kept us away because of the state of his Dad's house, or his Dad was keeping us away because he didn't want his mess discovered?" She suddenly gave a hoot of laughter. "That would have made Grace's job pretty hard, having to sift through rooms full of rubbish."

I chuckled along with her for a few seconds. "If indeed she really did take the key to get the house open. It seems pretty bizarre." I ran a finger along the top of the pew ahead of us, tracing the graceful grain of the wood. "She must have been a lot stronger than Matthew, being so much younger.

She could probably have just knocked on the door and over-powered him when he answered."

To that, Jude simply shrugged.

"Anyway, the kitchen doorway was the only one I saw open, although I think he must have slept in a room off the back of it. All the rest of the house is closed off. The Police had to get a big dumpster just to clear the newspapers out of the hallway. Heaven knows what else is inside."

As well as your dead mother-in-law.

14

LOOSE ENDS

WE PARTED COMPANY SOON AFTER – she to return to her motel and re-arrange childcare for little Sasha, and me intending to head off to my neglected office and a couple more hours of "Birds Can't Pee".

Jude had claimed she didn't know about Matthew's hoarding. She had a peculiar but reasonable excuse to be in Drizzle Bay. She said she had half-shares in a child, but not with its father. And she had a chip on her shoulder so big you could use it as an industrial doorstop. I wondered how much was true.

I needed to check the legal ramifications with Graham. I was pretty sure Sasha stood to inherit everything – including an elderly house and a classic Alfa Romeo or two.

But would Matthew's daughter-in-law get some of the benefit, or would the child's mother – the as-yet-unseen and avaricious Grace – be in luck? I suspected the latter, blood being thicker than water. Did either of them have enough motivation for murder? Or had someone else done the awful deed?

Even though it was Sunday I knew Graham might have popped into the office to do some work while it was quiet. I sat on one of the shopping center benches and pulled out my phone before I reached the car. The truck with the dogs had been replaced by a blue Honda, so there was no barking to disturb me, and there was a nice patch of sunshine to enjoy far enough away from the babble at the outdoor café tables. The aromas of coffee and daffodils swirled around me.

Graham answered promptly.

"Morning Jeepie," I said. "Sorry I dashed out so early without saying goodbye."

"It's years since you called me that. Brings back memories." He gave a gusty sigh. "How are you doing, Sis? Holding up okay?"

I probably sighed in return because he asked, "That bad, eh?"

"No – just complications. You said last night you'd looked into a divorce for Matthew Boatman. Does that mean you might have his last will and testament lodged in the office, too?"

He chuckled at my question. Maybe they didn't refer to it like that any longer. I heard him shuffling papers around, and much faster than I expected, he said, "Yes. I decided to come in and take a look after what you told me."

"Ummm... what about his wife? Did she leave a will too?"

Graham cleared his throat. "Why do I get the feeling you're meddling in things that don't concern you again?"

"I'm offering a trade," I said. "Info from you in return for info from me. And no-one else gets to hear about it for a while."

"Okay, I'll bite," Graham said, still making paper-shuffling noises. "Matthew left everything to his only son, James, and any issue thereafter – which is to say, any grandchildren he might have."

"And as the son is dead, it would be his six-year-old granddaughter. But what about the son's wife? And what if the little daughter is not the child of the wife?"

I heard a cup hit a saucer quite noisily, and pictured Graham about to take a sip of tea and then changing his mind with surprise. "So that's the trade?"

"Absolutely not. I have more than that. Did old Mrs Boatman leave a will?"

"As chance would have it," he said, shuffling paper again, "I have it right here. Her name was Emmy. Everything goes to... hmmm... strange... to any children she might have in the future. Nothing to Matthew."

I wondered if she'd had it prepared before he dragged her off to Africa in fragile health. Maybe it was intended as protection for her unborn child? I rubbed my nose. "Could that give Matthew a reason to kill her if she didn't leave anything to him? Always supposing she had anything to leave?"

"What an odd thing to think, Merry," Graham snapped.

"Longtime spouses can contest such things anyway." There was a drawn-out silence. "I think you'd better not go spreading stories like that," he finally said. "She died a long time ago, somewhere up north. I seem to recall they'd split up."

I let out a long, slow breath. "Thanks for telling me about the wills. I realize it's probably confidential information, and I suspect you're being nice to me because you know I had a bad shock yesterday."

"I'm sure it won't go any further," Graham said huffily.

"No. Absolutely not," I agreed. "But here's the thing. She didn't move away. She's still right here in Drizzle Bay – kind of mummified on Matthew's couch, and with a cross and artificial flowers all around her. They found her this morning."

Total silence.

"Are you still there?" I asked.

"Death Certificate," Graham muttered. "I wonder if it was ever issued?"

Trust him to follow the legal road and not the shock/horror route...

———

AFTER THAT, I really did go home and sit at my desk and put some effort into the next chapter of Elaine O'Blythe's misspelled, ungrammatical, but absolutely charming story. I emailed her some corrected pages and couldn't resist adding a note about my strange new menagerie and the title WPC Bess Moody had suggested.

Would 'The Orphan Cats of Paradise Road' ever be written? Might Siam be a suitable model for some of Elaine's fanciful watercolors? Should I ask Bess to send me some photos of him, in case? I'll bet he was already on Instagram, looking exotic and imperious and spoilt rotten. I should take photos of Peanut before she became Poppy Waitomo's pride and joy, and of Fifty and Skinnyblack and Onesie, too, because nothing was surer than that they'd be leaving as soon as I could persuade them out of the greenhouse to pastures new. It would be fun if Elaine decided she could use them.

From the sudden barking in the yard I surmised Graham was home and expecting lunch. I checked the time. Paul would be concluding the Family Service at Saint Agatha's any minute now. Heather was busy at The Café. Might my vicar be interested in home-made vegetable soup? There was a big pot of it in the fridge. I could grill and crumble some bacon in to make it more special.

I sent him a text, hoping he'd switched his phone to silent and it wasn't beeping in his pocket in front of the congregation.

He phoned me back pretty swiftly. "Sounds nicer than the crackers and cheese I was planning. Are you sure?"

"Of course I'm sure."

"Not that the soup will be better than the company," he hurriedly assured me.

I closed my eyes. "We'll have Graham, too."

"Sticking around to warn me off again, is he?" But I heard the humor in his voice.

I bit my lip. In for a penny, in for a pound. "When I thought about it later last night I wondered if he'd taken the dogs out to give us some privacy." I held my breath, wondering what he'd reply.

"I sometimes skive off to give Heather and Erik time on their own," he said. "Yes, let's hope he did. See you soon."

Huh! That hadn't fazed him. Seemed there might be hope for us romantically after all.

———

He departed at half past two to his Tots and Toddlers Teatime – apparently a mums and very young children get-together for the littlest members of his congregation to prevent them from disrupting the main Family Service. That might be something I could help him with if we ever actually got together, although Jude Boatman would be better at it than me.

It doesn't pay to think about people in case they appear, because there she suddenly was, strolling slow and bored under the shop verandas in the main street. She gave me a wave and half a smile, and looked hopeful I might stop. Belinda Butterfly's rack of late-season cut-price knitwear could wait.

"Would you like a coffee?" I asked.

She gathered up her bright hair into a ponytail and let go of it again. "Yes, but can we have a private chat first?" Her eyes were shifty and she seemed nervous.

Ooooh! Of course we could!

"Shell we sit in my car?" I waved a hand at my nearby aubergine pride and joy. "I guess you don't have a car here if you have the bike?"

She bobbed her head, which could have meant yes or no, so I beeped the doors unlocked and we sat.

She was silent for a couple of minutes, and I wondered if I should make an effort to start the conversation, but she was obviously wrestling with something so I let her choose when to begin.

"Grace did it."

I took a sudden breath, sucked something into my throat, and started coughing.

"How do you know?" I asked once I'd recovered.

"She met Jazzy at the Olympics. She's an archer. And..."

Crikey. Really? I sat there stunned until I managed to say, "They only said Matthew was shot."

"With one of her arrows," she muttered.

"How do you know?"

She sniffed, and not knowing whether she was likely to cry or sneeze I reached over and opened the compartment where I keep an opened pack of paper tissues.

She took one and blew her nose. "Because I saw the poor old boy. And the arrow. Before you did."

*Well thanks a million, ducky, leaving me to find him all over
again...*

She tipped her head back and breathed in hard. "When
Grace took the key on Thursday night – when I *presumed*
she'd taken the key, and we argued about it – she shot off in
our car like a madwoman. It was past midnight by then. As
luck would have it we'd arranged for Sasha to stay at her
little friend's house for the weekend." She gulped another
deep breath. "It took me a while to pack a bag for the bike,
and phone the mum and ask if she could take Sasha that
night instead. And lock up, and so on. But I set off for Drizzle
Bay and rode for hours through the night. I never passed
Grace, but she had quite a lead. Because I just *knew*." She
dabbed at her eyes.

"Anyway," she added after another huge breath, "I got
there, I saw the car further up the road, and the key was in
the front door of the house so I grabbed it and went in,
knowing Grace had to be somewhere close." She looked
across at me. "Sorry I pretended I didn't know what the place
was like inside. I was in a heck of a state. I found him sitting
at the table getting ready to give the cats their breakfast.
Animals milling around everywhere and yowling, and him
staring at me with an arrow in his back. Dead instantly, I'm
sure. She was a good shot." She scrubbed a hand across her
eyes. "Jazzy always had stories about how his father was a
hard man in Africa, and how the place was full of guns and
security. How he'd never let anyone get away with robbing
him, and would follow them to the ends of the earth to get

revenge. You know the kind of stuff. So that'd be why she shot him from outside."

"Why on earth didn't she think she'd be the obvious suspect? With the Olympics and all?"

Jude shook her head. "She was an odd person..."

You're telling me!

"I guess she thought she could do a disappearing act. Leave no trail. I left the door wide open, hoping that someone else would find him."

Yes, lucky Merry Summerfield did...

I tried not to let that influence me. "Did DS Bruce Carver talk with you yet?"

She nodding, biting her bottom lip.

"And you told him all of this?"

She worried at her lip some more and then shook her head.

"Why the heck not?" I exploded.

"They might have thought it was me. What if the neighbors heard the bike? Looked out their windows and saw me leaving? And never heard or saw her arrive earlier?"

"Oh for heaven's sake! Now you've given her a huge head start," I said crossly.

Jude hung her head. "Yes, she could be anywhere by now. But my guess is she would have driven straight back to Rotorua, grabbed all her things from the house, and kind of evaporated. It's... not her house. It's mine and Jazzy's. Mine now. She didn't pay rent – just sponged off us, having produced Sasha."

"What if she's taken Sasha?" Cruel of me, but it had to be asked.

"No." Jude shook her head. "When I phoned Kerry to ask if she could look after her for a while longer, I said to hide her if Grace turned up. And Kerry's a good friend. She said she was planning to take the girls out to her brother's farm for the day and they'd arrange to stay the night so the girls could feed the orphan lambs and calves in the morning. Grace wouldn't know where the farm is."

"Okay," I said, resigned to yet another chat with Bruce Carver. I dug out my phone.

"Ms Summerfield," he said wearily.

I breathed in. "I know who shot Matthew Boatman. It was Jude Boatman's housemate, Grace umm –"

"Goldfellow," Jude supplied in a small voice.

"Olympic archer," I added. "Jude's just told me all about it, and she's scared stiff, so I thought we might get a takeaway coffee from Iona and wait for you in my car. Unless you'd like me to drive her to you?"

———

I NEVER DID GET a look at Belinda's rack of late-season cut-price knitwear.

Instead, I galloped off to Paradise Road, hoping I'd timed it so there'd be enough light for feline photos. The dumpster was now piled high with old cardboard cartons and broken chairs. Presumably all the newspapers were finally out of the

hallway, and down the bottom of it. A couple of ancient suit-
cases were perched on top, lids flapping open. They
contained packages of porridge oats – no doubt full of
weevils – and rusty cans with remnants of labels saying
Italian tomatoes. It was a wonder they hadn't exploded or
eaten their way out after all those years. There was an enormous pile of rags and fabric remnants, including pairs of
large old white underpants which couldn't have fitted
Matthew for several decades, if ever. And enough Time
magazines to sink a ship.

It was so full they'd certainly need another dumpster. Or
two. A policeman was securing a big net over the top so
nothing could blow away in the blustery wind. Yes, Paradise
Road didn't need an invasion of old underpants in the night.
I'd lay odds a truck would be by first thing next morning to
take this one away and bring another.

I gave him a cheery grin. "For the cats," I called, patting
the pack of Fortune Kitty, now sporting silver duct tape over
its hole.

"Right you are," he yelled, trying to hold a corner of the
net and confine rubbish at the same time. I took pity on him
and grabbed the net for a while so he could pursue a big
yellowing scenic calendar which was trying to flap its way to
freedom. This of course gave me time to check for other
interesting items of garbage. OMG – part of a very old
Christmas tree. And a crumpled Abba poster that might even
be worth money if someone ironed it flat. Although... what
were those bugs scurrying out from between the folds? Had

they been eating it? Dusty old shoes. Ancient threadbare slippers – those tartan ones, and with a hole where a big toe had poked through. Many pairs of both. Rusty cake-tins.

The cop waved his thanks and I turned away. Knowing I'd get nothing but feline tails and backs if I appeared with food, I set the Fortune Kitty pack down on the empty patch of concrete beside the garage and pulled out my phone. Then I walked slowly and quietly around to the greenhouse.

They heard me of course. Onesie, looking like a large lump of coal, opened his eye and immediately became more photogenic. Peanut, who had somehow snaffled all of the largest bed, did a big stretch and rolled over to display a pretty fluffy tummy. Fifty was squashed up against Skinny-black. Neither took any notice of me so I got a nice cuddly shot. There was no sign of Whiteguy, which was good. The moment I retrieved the food, though, it was animation central. Cats unwound and unraveled and stood and yowled, demanding dinner in a variety of tones – none very polite.

Sadly there was no-one human I could ask questions of. I suppose everyone needs a day off sometimes, and it was Sunday after all. By the time I'd fed and watered the cats even the net-over-the-dumpster cop had gone.

I returned home to cook dinner for Graham. He'd decided to open a bottle of Pinot Noir once he smelled the meaty fumes from the beef and veg casserole, and we spent a happy evening together – me thinking of Paul conducting Evensong along at the Burkeville Chapel, and Graham choosing to watch one of those American TV programs about whether it was murder or suicide.

I flopped down beside him and we found we'd polished off so much of the bottle that we poured out the last half-glass each before each dozing off against each other like Fifty and Skinnyblack – or indeed, Manny and Dan the spaniels who'd taken over the mat in front of the wood burner.

Good heavens, the woman's fingerprints weren't on the shotgun and the husband's were. There was no way it was suicide, even though we found we'd missed the ending once we woke up.

And this, of course, got me thinking about what had happened to old Mrs Boatman as I changed for bed. Murder or suicide? Or natural causes? If she really was as desiccated as Marian Wick had claimed, how would anyone be able to tell? What sort of coroner's report would be possible after all this time?

Unless there were bullets, of course, but I couldn't picture Matthew with a gun, despite Jazzy's stories. Or maybe it wasn't Matthew?

15

INTO THE SPARKLY PIT OF HELL

THE CATS DIDN'T GET QUITE SUCH an early breakfast on Monday. However, duty done, I returned home and got stuck into the electrical catalog I'd mentioned to Paul on Friday evening. As a freelance editor I need to accept some jobs that are delightful – like Elaine O'Blythe's lovely children's stories – and some that are the pits – like electrical catalogs pieced together by someone whose first language isn't English.

What a slog. Even finding the correct spellings for some of the components took ages, but unraveling the descriptions and rewriting them so they'd make sense to English speakers was curiously satisfying once my brain resigned itself to the task.

The wind buffeted the house, gusting through the trees, whipping spume from the waves over the road, and rattling the guttering. I hoped they'd achieved the dumpster swap-over without any paper escaping – and that they didn't find any more to flap away today.

I kept myself sane by visiting Iona's for lunch – and who should be there grabbing two takeaway coffees but Detective Marian Wick.

"You did it again," she said, pretending displeasure. But a slight grin quirked the corners of her mouth. It was hard to be annoyed with someone who'd connected as intimately as we had, even if she'd left stray bruises on me with her bony hips.

"Do you think I have a sympathetic face?" I asked. "People just randomly tell me things sometimes."

"Don't worry about it. We have to catch her yet."

"By 'her' I presumed she meant Grace Goldfellow, because the lethal ex-Olympian had indeed drifted away like smoke. Bruce Carver had reluctantly told me her car hadn't been seen on the main highway anywhere between Drizzle Bay and Rotorua. No cellphone pings had given her location away. I'd Googled her to see what she looked like, but the only photos were sporty ones from years ago. Then, she was a lean, hawk-faced, dark-haired woman with a killer tan. Now she might be a tubby, pasty-faced blonde for all I knew. I daresay Jude would have passed on an accurate description to the Police before she left to retrieve her daughter.

The more I'd thought about it, the more likely it had seemed those girls at the Burkeville were friends of Grace Goldfellow's. Maybe they were hiding her? That hissed comment of 'Gray said not to tell,' kept floating around my brain.

Cat-feeding time rolled around, and once again I drove the three blocks to Matthew's old house, thinking I'd be able to walk there soon if the bag of Fortune Kitty kept emptying out at its current rate.

I was wearing an old pink jersey today, and had rolled my unruly hair up under a matching knitted hat, perfect for keeping it out of my eyes in the gale.

To my surprise Vinny Waitomo was waiting for me, cat-carrier at the ready. He beamed when he saw me. "I couldn't keep it a secret from Poppy," he said. "She wants it before her birthday if that's okay?"

"Absolutely fine," I said, relieved to have got another puss off the property. "Get the door open and see if you can scoop Peanut out from the feeding frenzy." Already my shins were being bumped by hard little heads, and my jeans pawed and patted.

I released the top of the bag and the mewing increased in volume. My furry crew fell to eating, and Vinny decided to wait until Peanut had been fed before attempting the cat-napping. "She's going to be a while in the car," he said.

What a nice man. Peanut would surely be happy with Vinny and Poppy.

I left him to it, waved goodbye, and carried the Fortune Kitty around toward the gate. On the way I saw the padlock to the back door of the garage was swinging loose again, so I set the pack on the ground and back-tracked. Might I get a better look inside this time? Was it also going to be full of rubbish like the house? Were there two expensive cars or one? My curiosity sometimes knows no bounds. There were still police working inside the house so I knew I'd better be fast.

I stepped inside and waited for my eyes to adjust to the darkness. Seconds later I heard footsteps behind me, and took an involuntary step forward. My foot connected with fresh air, and then what felt like a solid step. Ouch! I felt around for another. Yes... In the nick of time I bobbed down and bumped on my jeans-clad bottom down into an inspection pit beneath the car. Talk about a fright. I gasped in a deep breath and froze rigid. Maybe if I was very quiet whoever it was would do what they needed and go away again?

I was no stranger to automotive inspection pits. There used to be one in the garage at home until Dad had it boarded over when Ten Ton Smedley at Drizzle Bay Auto Services took on our car maintenance. Mostly the cars go up on his amazing hydraulic hoist so he can check everything underneath them, but he has a massive pit for trucks because they're too heavy to lift up.

Crikey – what now? The person didn't seem to be walking anywhere, but their shadow was moving very slightly against the sun so I knew they were still there. Then the shadow disappeared and I heard quiet footsteps beside the car. Whoever belonged to them kept walking forward, so I took the opportunity to raise my head and squint around. I could see better now I was more used to the darkness. Above me, a car gave total concealment. To each side there was dim light. And on the right – the house side – the wall of the pit had a darker rectangular shape. It almost looked like a door. I reached across and gave it a tentative push. To my astonishment it swung aside on silent hinges.

I scrambled across to it as quietly as I could. My feet told me there was no further drop, so I inched my way into the strange secret space and maneuvered the door closed behind me. I decided I had to be under the ugly slab of concrete beside the garage. The one that served no purpose. But pulling out my phone and shining the light around cautiously I saw it formed the rough roof to a small room. A room with one chair, a desk with an interesting-looking lamp, and shelves along its back edge. In those shelves lurked an assortment of small boxes and bags.

On top of the desk a length of black velvet had been unrolled.

On top of the velvet lay a sprinkle of glittering stones.

My breath hitched sharply, and only the thought of being discovered prevented me from whooping with glee. I clutched my throat, willing myself to stay silent.

Diamonds. Diamonds. Diamonds. Lots of them.

And who knew what else was concealed in all those little boxes and bags?

I played my torch across the river of sparkles, shading it with my hand, and praying the light couldn't be seen by whoever was up above. But my luck ran out. Something large arrived in the pit, and whoever it was had no qualms about keeping quiet or dark.

The door swung open and I was dazzled by light. "Found you, Jude," a gloating female voice said, while the light kept me blinded. "And look at this – Jazzy wasn't joking. His old Dad really did have money to burn. What else has he got here?"

Jude? Why did she think I was Jude?

A hand reached out and I flinched as far backward as I could. Which wasn't much, but at least out of reach of its grasp, because the owner seemed far more intent on the jewels than the trembling person who had led the way into the underground lair.

I watched as the hand grabbed one of the boxes, flipped off the top with a careless finger, and tossed a flash of blue-green onto the velvet. The light played over the sea of color.

"Aqua," the voice said reverently. "Nice ones. Big ones."

I had the ridiculous thought that if this was Grace Gold-fellow at least there wasn't room to use a bow and arrow down here. I dared to shine my phone-torch at her, and sure enough, hawk-like features, dark hair, not so far removed from her photos on the internet.

"Switch it off!" she snapped. "You don't need to see me now. You won't ever be seeing me again."

Unfortunately this didn't mean she'd be grabbing the booty and running. It meant she'd be taking care of me first and ensuring my silence with an evil-looking knife she wore on her belt. As she'd already killed Matthew, another body wouldn't matter. Especially one which she could leave concealed in this nasty place until she was far, far away.

She waved the knife and the light flashed off the blade as I cowered, defenseless, in front of her.

Graham, I love you. Be happy with Susan.

Paul, we could have made a go of it.

But as she lunged, a huge brown hand grabbed her arm, pulling it back out of harm's way.

"Drop it," Vinny Waitomo growled. "Game's up Sweetheart."

I heard something pop in Grace's arm. The knife hit the floor with a clang. I clutched at the wall to try and stay upright. And Grace folded up, moaning with pain and howling with fury.

Then I fell onto the floor too – with relief, and disbelief, and because my legs didn't work any longer.

"Vinny!" I quavered as Grace continued to vent her annoyance beside me. "You sounded like an American TV cop! How did you get down here so quietly?"

He beamed at me in the fitful light cast by my phone, and kicked the knife in under the desk. "Will that go brighter?" he asked, planting a big boot in the center of Grace's back once he'd pushed her down flat onto the dirty floor.

I scrambled up, brushing at the knees of my jeans, and tried the light on the desk.

"Ooo-eee!" he murmured, casting a quick eye over the trail of diamonds and aquamarines it illuminated. "So that's what she was after?" He bent and grabbed Grace's uninjured wrist, pulling her arm up behind her to a position that couldn't have been comfortable.

"Softly, softly," he said to me. "No-one takes any notice of a man in uniform standing around looking bored. But he sees. It's his job. He sees everything that goes on."

Grace let out an enraged groan, and he took no notice.

"And you saw *her*?" I asked.

"I saw her sneaking through the hedge when I was on duty Saturday night and they needed the house guarded after the old boy was murdered. Saw her come skulking up to try the garage door, like you did. And I wondered what was in here that young ladies might be so interested in."

Grace muttered something extremely rude.

So she'd still been around the property, determined to search every inch of it?

"I only wanted a look at the vintage Italian cars," I said. "Ten Ton Smedley says they're worth a bomb."

"But not as much as those, eh?" Vinny said, giving the glittering stones a closer inspection. He glanced at all the small boxes and bags. "You reckon there are more?"

"Maybe hundreds," I said. "He probably smuggled them in from Africa, years ago. He used to live there."

"What a waste," Vinny said. "Those beautiful cars, all

these diamonds, and he lived in a house like that, full of rubbish."

"With his wife lying dead on the sofa for years," I couldn't help adding.

Grace made a gargling noise. Vinny bugged his eyes.

"I'll phone Bruce Carver," I said, thinking he'd be pleased to have another crim in the bag.

EPILOGUE

"Ms Summerfield," he said. It still sounded as though the weight of the world was on his shoulders.

"We need you here at Paradise Road," I said. "That's if you're not already here somewhere. And please bring handcuffs."

"Really?" he asked.

"Yes, really. The security man and I have Grace Goldfellow restrained."

Well, it was Vinny doing all the restraining but he didn't seem the sort of man to argue, and I was helping by phoning.

Bruce cleared his throat. "Putting you on speaker for Detective Wick's benefit," he said. And then, no doubt to her because he dropped his volume, "They've got Goldfellow."

"Come to the back door of the garage," I instructed. There's an inspection pit under the first car, and it leads into a little room. Although there won't be space down here for me and her and Vinny and the two of you as well."

"There in sixty seconds," he snapped. He really didn't sound as pleased as I'd hoped he would.

———

GRACE GOLDFELLOW WAS SWIFTLY REMOVED to have her arm attended to, and to face eventual trial.

I finally worked out why she'd called me 'Jude' in the secret gem store. Jeans and a pink jersey. And that hat to keep my hair under control in the gale. If she'd seen my blonde hair instead of Jude's bright red curls it might have been a different story. Or would it? No – she still would have pulled the knife to get her hands on the glitter.

I've no idea what will happen to all the gemstones. I guess their ownership will be thoroughly investigated and either little Sasha will inherit them or they'll be seized by the Customs Department – or whoever's in charge of such things.

The beautiful old cars will definitely be Sasha's, although they'll be even more vintage by the time she's old enough to drive. In the meantime Jude now has the full-time daughter she's yearned for, and I gather she's selling the Ducati motorcycle so she can ferry Sasha around in Alfa Romeo style and safety.

Graham told me in confidence that Matthew had made a generous bequest to the Drizzle Bay Animal Shelter so his cats could be looked after for the rest of their natural lives, and another to Saint Agatha's parish with the stipulation it went toward building a new Church Hall 'as a place of companionship.' Lurline and Paul will both be thrilled once it's made official.

Peanut has been renamed Rosebud, and Poppy thinks Vinny Waitomo is the best Dad in the world.

Scans showed no bullets or broken bones in poor old Emmy Boatman. Maybe she really did die of natural causes and Matthew couldn't bear to be parted from her? We'll never know. They were buried together in a peaceful corner of Saint Agatha's churchyard.

———

A FORTNIGHT after the turbulence had settled, Paul took me to The Burkeville again, but this time there were no inquisitive customers. We were in the private dining room of the big house Erik and John jointly owned. Erik had returned from whatever mysterious assignment he'd been on. Heather and Graham had both been invited, too. It was almost the same crowd who'd witnessed Erik requesting that Heather stayed in New Zealand 'for him' all those months ago.

Delicious nibbles were set out on the big table, and once we were all assembled, drinking and grazing happily, Erik rose, and Heather stood up beside him.

Here we go at last, I thought, and sure enough...

"They're very good bubbles," he said, nodding toward the

bottles. "Chosen for a special toast." He slid an arm around Heather's waist. "Life's going to change for the Burkeville Boys."

"And the Burkeville Babe," she added with a cheeky grin.

Eric dropped a kiss on her hair. "Yeah – and the Burkeville Babe." He looked across at Paul. "I've already made my intentions clear toward your sister, but now I'm in a position to set proper plans in place. I've been sorting out a family situation in the US. None of you except Jawn will know I had a seriously ill wife until a couple of weeks ago. A wife in name only for longer than the time I've been here, but I don't walk out on my responsibilities."

He gazed at the rest of us almost as though we might argue, but we were riveted to our chairs with excitement and hope.

"So," he continued, "Ms Heather here has consented to be my wife as soon as we can respectably swing it." He looked down at her with eyes lit with love. "In fact we already brought the ring some time ago, and from tonight she can wear it, because we made sure it was the right size, and as long as she hasn't changed her mind...?"

I adored that slight suggestion he thought she might yet escape his clutches.

Heather showed no doubts though. She simply held out her left hand toward him and wiggled her fingers encouragingly.

"Ah, Babe," he said. "Long wait, but so worth it."

Then he surprised us all by lifting the lid off the sugar

bowl and producing a small velvet-covered box from inside it.

The diamond sparkled as brightly as any I'd seen on Matthew Boatman's secret table, and Heather smiled softly as he slid the platinum band onto her finger.

"Heather and Erik," Paul said, lifting his glass. We happily joined him in the toast as they sealed their official partnership with a very hot kiss.

"Aaaaand there's more news," John drawled once the congratulations and hugs had died away. "As you can see, these two will want a heap of privacy so I'll be moving out in a while. Some of you know I was trying to buy that wreck of a cottage at The Point." He gazed around jubilantly. "I finally got it!"

"Isobel Crombie's old place," I said. "Where I first met you when I was looking after Itsy and Fluffy. Has her sister decided to sell up and move on?"

"Yep," he agreed. "It's in bad shape, but the location is magic. The reno needs to be very softly-softly though, so those official building folks don't see I'm turning it into a California surfing shack until it's too late to reverse the process."

We all laughed at that. John enjoys quality; a 'shack' it would never be once he'd had his way with it.

"Jawn's new home," Erik said, lifting his glass again.

"John's new home," the rest of us chorused.

"And this," Heather said, pointing at Paul, "means you'll have a vacancy for a good cook and freelance editor if you ever decide you're past the PTSD and in a fit state to join the real world."

Paul's eyes shot wide open. "Heather!" he objected. "Not your business…"

She smiled serenely. "Someone needs to push you, or you'll never be ready." She turned toward me. "Will he, Merry?"

"*Definitely* not your business," I retorted, although I caught the ghost of a smile on Paul's lips.

Attempting to take the attention off me, I raised my glass toward Graham. "And if I *was* to move out, you should see if you and Susan Hammond can do better than your occasional sex-nights."

"Merry!" Graham snapped, a tide of pink rising up his face. "We don't have occasional sex-nights!"

I tapped the side of my nose. "Brother, you've been having them for a couple of years. But are you telling me you have quite frequent ones instead?"

That was enough to make us all dissolve into guffaws and giggles. The pressure was off, the steam escaping. It was a happy night.

THE END

A NOTE FROM KRISTIE

Thank you so much for reading the third Merry Summerfield cozy mystery. They're real fun to write, and leave me with a brain stuffed with details and hoping I have everything in the right place.

A very special 'thank you' to my awesome ARC team. Some of you have been traveling along with me for years, might have left for a while because of health issues or family circumstances, and then returned. You're so valuable to me, and your keen eyes and inquiring brains are much appreciated. After the typos you find, the grammar you query, the pertinent questions you ask, and the suggestions you offer, I think we turn out a pretty good product. And even when you're far more interested in the story than the details, your reviews conveying enjoyment are solid gold and help keep sales ticking over. Hugs to you all!

I began my working life as an advertising copywriter at my local radio station in Hawkes Bay, New Zealand. Once I'd saved up enough to go travelling I lived in Italy and London. Then I returned to my capital city of Wellington and worked in TV, radio again, several advertising agencies, and then spent happy years as a retail ad manager. Totally hooked on fabrics, I followed this by going into business with my husband, Philip, as a curtain installer, working for some of the city's top designers. Quite a turnaround! It was finally time to write fiction. In twenty years I haven't fallen off my ladder once through drifting off into creating the current book, but I've certainly seen some beautiful homes and met wonderful people.

To see all my titles, including my cozies, go to krispearson.com. Click on the book covers to see more. But be warned – the contemporary romances I've written under my real name of Kris Pearson are totally different from the Merry Summerfield mysteries.

To see only the Kristie Klewes cozies, go to kristieklews.com

Now read on for a taste of number four – Body! They Barked.

SHOPPING FOR TROUBLE

Wow, they're big! And hairy! If pet-sitters were paid by the pound or kilogram I'd be making a fortune this time. I'm in charge of two huge German Shepherds.

Hi – I'm Merry Summerfield, freelance book editor, wanting to escape from the enjoyable but predictable company of my brother, Graham.

Just now and again, you understand.

So I came up with a scheme to get a little freedom and some extra pocket money as a house and pet sitter. The dogs and cats of Drizzle Bay get company and regular meals. If there are houseplants or a veggie patch needing water, I'm your girl. And I can carry right on working on my trusty laptop.

Today I've deserted the all-too-wordy novel I'm currently editing – a Spanish Jane Austen vampire saga. Honestly, these mixed-trope things are all the rage and you wouldn't believe some of the themes people come up with.

I'm trying to erect antiquated trestle tables in the vacant shop next to Winston Bamber's classy art gallery. My large new charges, Fire and Ice, are watching attentively.

I'd caught my thumb in one of the uncooperative table stands and was sucking it to dull the pain when the vicar's sister trotted through the open door and gave a loud squawk. Either Fire or Ice sprang up with an answering woof. Heather clutched a hand to her pink-shirted bosom, and her very pretty eyes did a huge boggle.

"Arrghhh!" was the most she managed to say for a moment or two.

"Sit!" I snapped at the offending Shepherd, and to my surprise, he did. "Good boyyyyyy," I added in an enthusiastic tone, hoping we were making progress together.

"What –?" Heather asked. "Um – what are you doing? And why the dogs?"

That surprised me. "Didn't Erik say?" Of all people, he should have told her. They're finally getting married as soon as they can arrange it.

He's Erik Jacobsen of the Burkeville Bar and Café, and he's whipped off to wherever he used to live in the USA to attend to some details following the death of a divorced wife we never knew he had. His off-sider, John Bonnington, has disappeared on mysterious and urgent Black Ops assassin business. I might be assuming too much there, but John is definitely into secret stuff. I've seen photos of him in scuba gear looking very shifty by unknown boats. And, in person, in board shorts, dripping wet, long bones hung about with the hardest muscles you've ever seen. Not that I was looking too intently, you understand.

Anyway...

I walked a few steps toward Heather. "I'm doing a pet-and-house sitting job for Erik and John. They're both away at the same time, which I can't remember happening in the years I've known them." I put my sore thumb back into my mouth, and then, fearing I'd look like an overgrown baby, pulled it out again.

Either Fire or Ice gave a gusty sigh.

"They reckoned their staff would have plenty to do keeping the Bar and Café going without feeding and walking these two as well. I'm in the guest bedroom."

"Of their house?" she asked rather sharply.

"Yes, of course." (Their very nice beachfront house along in Burkeville on the main highway north of Drizzle Bay.)

"Why didn't they ask me?" she demanded.

Well, how would I know?

"Probably thought you had enough on your plate with your job at Iona's, house-keeping for Paul, and getting ready for the wedding. And your mother's up-coming visit, of course," I said, thinking rapidly on my sneaker-clad feet.

That calmed her down a little. "I knew he'd be gone until next week," she said, obviously referring to her fiancé, Erik – shorter than John, and maybe older than John, although now I know them a lot better I suspect it's his thick, prematurely white hair that makes me think that. He's certainly amazingly fit, and equally at home behind the Burkeville's bar or ferrying tourists around in his helicopter.

I tried for a gentle, consoling tone. "Given the circumstances – ex-wife and so on – maybe he didn't want to talk about it too much?"

"Angie-Jo," she muttered. "Never a word about her until she died, but I knew something was holding him back."

"Do you think she was sick, or was it a road accident, or what?" Very nosy of me, I know, but sometimes it's best to get the proper picture so you can comment. Or not, depending on the situation.

Heather shook her head. "Haven't a clue. Didn't know she even existed, until she didn't." She shot another watchful glance at the dogs. The dogs watched her in return. I'd tied them to the iron uprights on the small counter that used to hold a big roll of brown paper when this was a haberdashery store. Many years ago.

"I've arranged the morning off," she added. And when I inspected her properly I saw she was very nicely made up, with her hair loose, and looking nothing like she does while working at Iona's café. "Trying on wedding dresses," she added with a soft smile. "Belinda at Brides by Butterfly let me know yesterday she was planning to unpack new stock last night and said there were some I simply had to see."

Oh good – it sounded as though the discovery of Erik's first wife hadn't put her off. "More fun than this," I said, waving a hand around the dirty old shop.

If all goes according to plan, and Vicar Paul McCreagh ever escapes from the Afghanistan-induced PTSD bunker he's stuck in, Heather and I might become sisters-in-law. And I'd love that, but there's a bit of water to flow under the bridge first.

"So what are you actually doing?" She wrinkled her nose.

Yes, it's a rather smelly old place, having been mostly shut up for ages. Musty and mushroomy. It needs a good airing out before I can possibly hold any sort of literary workshop in it. And maybe I'll squirt some French Begonia air fragrancer around, too.

"Well," I said, giving my jeans a hitch because they have the hidden wide elastic inside the top and it never quite holds them up properly. "It all started with Lord Drizzle's family history. He enjoyed writing it so much that he talked Lady Zinnia into doing the same about the art groups in the area. And then young David surprised us by mentioning some science fiction stories he'd written."

"Probably an escape from his awful mother," Heather inserted.

"Maybe."

But she's dead now, poor thing, and he's found a happy home at Drizzle Farm. Jim Drizzle makes sure he gets to school, not that he seems to need any encouragement, and Lady Zin sees he's well fed. He lives in an old house-bus parked there. And OMG, I'd been glad he did, but that's a story for another day. He'll be leaving for university soon.

"Anyway," I continued, "one thing has led to another. The

coast seems to be full of people who want to write something and don't know where to start. Or have already written it and want to know if it's any good and what to do next. Jim keeps referring them to me."

"He's hard to ignore, isn't he?" Heather said. And then added, "I tried writing a novel once, with recipes."

I waited for her to continue but she simply shook her head. "It was rubbish."

Maybe it wasn't, though? Perhaps I could persuade her to join the soon-to-be critique group?

"Are you in a rush?" I asked. I would be if I was intending to try on wedding dresses but she could always turn me down.

"No, not really." She surprised me by walking slowly across to the Shepherds and holding out a hand to be sniffed. It got a full-on lathering from two long pink tongues. "Urk!" she exclaimed. "Look at that dribble. Now I'm all wet. But I guess I need to get to know them better if I'm going to live with them."

Was she picturing them flopped down on the hearth-rug in front of Erik and John's fireplace while she knitted baby booties? Nope – they're outdoor dogs, with high-tech kennels in their own yard behind the café. Anyway, John is quietly renovating an old beach cottage he plans to move into eventually.

I tried not to laugh. "Well, if you're really not in too much of a hurry, can you give me a hand with these tables?"

The old trestles had been donated by Lucy Stephenson,

the very thin and very nice head teacher at the Burkeville Secondary School. If you're not from New Zealand I should probably explain that the pupils start there at age twelve or thirteen and the best ones go on to university after maybe another five years' education.

"No trouble," Heather said. "Are you setting up a writing class?"

"Kind of," I agreed, indicating one of the trestle stands. "We can start with this across the back. They're some of the old tables from the school. The new ones have fancy fold down legs, and these were going begging. So I begged."

It took us only a few minutes working together. Stands lined up, tops lowered on, and then we stood reading the very creative graffiti. Oh dear. I was going to have to cover them with something...

"You should join us," I said. "Either with your old book, or to try writing a new one."

She rolled her eyes at me. "That'll be the day!"

Darn – she would have been fun. "Okay. Thank you. Go and enjoy your dresses. Let me know if you find something gorgeous." I gave her a quick hug before she bustled off.

So. This shop. It's been empty for ages. When I gave it a thorough sweep I could see it had mice, although what they ate was a mystery. I've put down half a dozen of those little plastic box-traps that don't actually hurt them. If anyone goes in after the cheese then I'll set them free – way down the beach where they can take their chances with seagulls or feral cats. Would a seagull eat a mouse?

And in the meantime, there being nothing to steal except some old tables that were too heavy to carry off without transport, I'd decided to leave the front and back doors wide open and take my hairy charges for a beach walk. Hopefully the flow of air in through one doorway and out through the other would have it smelling better by the time we returned.

I unbolted the back door and found a bare alley running behind Winston Bamber's gallery. A big green plastic wheelie bin, a few dead leaves and a brick were all it contained. I secured the door by holding it open with the brick. The front door was easy enough, too. A hook slid into a loop and held it steady.

Fire and Ice sensed action would be following, and leaped to their feet, shaking their heads so the buckles and tags on their collars rattled. "Yes, boys," I said. "Walkies." No way in the world does John ever say 'walkies'. I might be exaggerating if I said they rolled their eyes, but they certainly gave me big doggie grins with their tongues hanging out, and I'm sure they looked at each other mirthfully and sent silent messages about the easy-to-con woman who thought she was in charge of them.

I hitched their leads from the old counter fittings, patted my sweatshirt to make sure John's special whistle was hanging there between my D cups, and off we went. The whistle is a stupid thing. I can't hear it, no matter how hard I blow it. Fire and Ice certainly can though; it gets their attention instantly.

Drizzle Bay looked most attractive in its early summer

guise. The springtime daffodils in the tubs along the main street had been replaced with cute little conifers. The shop windows sparkled. Saint Agatha's garden borders now boasted pretty clumps of lavender, so Vicar Paul had been busy yet again.

And speak of the devil – or the vicar – there he was, striding toward me, dark hair ruffled by the breeze, teeth and dog-collar both shining white in the sun. I had the leads in my right hand so Paul chose my left side.

"Bigger animals than I generally see you with?"

He was definitely after information, so I sent him a fairly sweet smile and said, "John's away for a few days."

I wondered what he'd say to that, and sure enough his eyebrows rose and he gaped a bit. "Are you house-sitting for him? Where's Erik?"

"Gone to the States. Sorting out legal stuff."

He nodded along, and then asked, "To do with the wife?"

Okay, Heather is his sister, and he was no doubt interested in the man she was planning to marry, but I didn't greatly like his tone. Just to wind him up, I said, "I guess. Heather didn't seem to know much about his trip."

Paul's teeth disappeared. "You've seen her this morning?"

"Yes, she gave me a hand to set up some trestle tables in the old shop."

"So she's not working?"

Wow – that was pretty fast. "No – she's trying on wedding dresses."

He chewed his bottom lip for a while. "Mmm... I thought

she was being secretive about something. Avoided having breakfast with me. Dashed out yelling goodbye but giving no details."

"Probably didn't think you'd be interested," I said, knowing he would indeed be *intensely* interested.

He coughed. "Yes, maybe. So what's happening in the shop?"

See what I mean? Likes to know everything, but maybe it comes with the job and he simply feels the need to keep up with all of his parishioners.

By now we'd reached the pedestrian crossing leading over to the beach. The dogs lifted their muzzles and sniffed at the ocean air, their sensitive noses no doubt finding all sorts of interesting scents. Dead fish, discarded food, other dogs' musky markers... Euw.

We walked across the road together, Fire and Ice now tugging at their leads. It was all I could do to hold them back. "Not yet! Not yet!" I gasped.

———

Buy **BODY THEY BARKED** now to read the rest.